Billie Bradley and the School Mystery

Or, The Girl From Oklahoma

Janet D. Wheeler

Alpha Editions

This edition published in 2021

ISBN : 9789354941177

Design and Setting By
Alpha Editions
www.alphaedis.com
Email - info@alphaedis.com

As per information held with us this book is in Public Domain.
This book is a reproduction of an important historical work. Alpha Editions
uses the best technology to reproduce historical work in the same manner
it was first published to preserve its original nature. Any marks or number
seen are left intentionally to preserve its true form.

Contents

CHAPTER I AT LAKE MOLATA — - 1 -

CHAPTER II A DESPERATE FIX — - 6 -

CHAPTER III EDINA TO THE RESCUE — - 10 -

CHAPTER IV BATTLE — - 14 -

CHAPTER V A PUBLIC REBUKE — - 18 -

CHAPTER VI BILLIE IS LOYAL — - 23 -

CHAPTER VII A TALE OF RICHES — - 29 -

CHAPTER VIII BILLIE AGAINST HER WORLD — - 33 -

CHAPTER IX THE EXPERIMENT — - 37 -

CHAPTER X A TRIP TO TOWN — - 41 -

CHAPTER XI EDINA GETS HER HAIR CUT — - 46 -

CHAPTER XII A PERFECT DAY — - 52 -

CHAPTER XIII EDINA SCORES — - 55 -

CHAPTER XIV AN OLD ENEMY — - 59 -

CHAPTER XV AN UNEXPECTED DUCKING — - 65 -

CHAPTER XVI FIGHTING FOR LIFE — - 70 -

CHAPTER XVII THE MYSTERIOUS LETTER — - 76 -

CHAPTER XVIII THE GIFT CLUB — - 79 -

CHAPTER XIX A DREADFUL DISCOVERY — - 83 -

CHAPTER XX THE ACCUSATION	- 88 -
CHAPTER XXI EVIDENCE PILES UP	- 93 -
CHAPTER XXII A RIOT	- 97 -
CHAPTER XXIII DAN LARKIN REMEMBERS	- 103 -
CHAPTER XXIV A SMASHING SET	- 108 -
CHAPTER XXV CAUGHT—CONCLUSION	- 113 -

CHAPTER I
AT LAKE MOLATA

"MY, but it's good to get back!"

The statement came from Billie Bradley. She gazed upon the ivy-covered towers of the boarding school with genuine affection.

Three Towers Hall was an impressive building, set amidst gracious, well-tended lawns on the borders of one of the prettiest and most picturesque lakes in that part of the country. From its gates students flocked in gay anticipation of vacation and good times at the end of the spring term, to return, more soberly, but with a refreshed and brightened outlook, to take up their studies at the beginning of the fall semester.

Such a time had come again to Billie Bradley and her two close chums, Violet Farrington and Laura Jordon. After a particularly interesting and adventure-filled summer, they had returned to their beloved seat of learning, eager for work and with renewed and heightened ideals.

Now they stood on the borders of the lake, looking toward Three Towers Hall through a lane of trees that made flickering shadows on the lawn. Idly, they speculated on the future.

"I'd feel better," observed Vi, "if I hadn't that condition in math to make up. It worries me."

"It would," agreed Laura. "I mean, it would have worried me so much that if it had been my condition, I'd have made it up during the summer instead of waiting until fall, when goodness knows the work is hard enough, anyway."

"It's easy enough for you to criticize," said Vi, a shade resentfully. "You take all your studies at a run, while all I can do is to hobble."

"Of course, not everyone can have a brain like mine," murmured Laura, with a mischievous grin.

"Besides, what time have I had this summer for study?" Vi persisted. "Between treasure hunts and mysteries and such things, I've had my hands full."

"You should have found time," returned Laura, pursing her mouth primly in mischievous imitation of Miss Phelps, their new mathematics teacher. "Where there's a will, there's a way."

Vi shrugged her shoulders petulantly.

"Well, if you are going to be so disagreeable—" She left the sentence unfinished and turned toward the Hall.

Billie awoke from the reverie that had been occupying her secret thoughts; awoke in time to seize a fold of Vi's abbreviated skirt and hold it firmly between thumb and forefinger.

"Laura's insulting me," said Vi, with a wavering smile. "I'll not stay."

"Don't be foolish," laughed Billie. "Laura insults everybody. It's just her way. But she never means anything by it."

"I'm going up to the house to study math," persisted Vi.

"No you're not," said Billie. "You are going for a walk with Laura and me back of the lake and pick goldenrod. Miss Walters likes it in her office and it would be nice in the dorm. Come along."

"But I must study math!" wailed Vi, beginning to weaken. "Honestly, Billie, you don't know how it worries me. It has me scared stiff."

"Well, we'll go and pick goldenrod first and then I'll help you with your math. How will that do?"

"Excellently, thanks," said Vi, with a sigh of relief. When Billie helped with "math," or anything else, she really helped, explaining each step and making everything as clear as day. Vi had wished, many a time, that she had Billie's head for "math."

The three girls took the footpath to the right of the lake, the path that climbed steadily until it came out on a high ridge of ground overlooking both Three Towers Hall and Boxton Military Academy, the boys' school directly across the lake from the Hall.

Billie Bradley and her chums knew that on this ridge grew goldenrod, flaming, golden patches of it. The sight of it always fascinated them. As Billie once had said, it seemed as though the sun had touched the earth and become entangled in the weeds.

"It was some time before it could untangle itself and get back in the heavens where it belonged," Billie had concluded her whimsical fancy. "The result was—goldenrod!"

Now, as they made their way toward this higher ground, the girls continued to discuss the events of the past few days, the renewal of acquaintanceship with old school friends, the excitement and interest of meeting and "looking over" the newcomers to Three Towers Hall.

"The new girls seem a rather commonplace lot," observed Laura. She paused by the wayside to pick a lace flower and stuck it jauntily over one ear revealed by a very short bob. "Just the usual smattering; some shy, some bold, all somewhat excited by finding themselves at boarding school."

"Can you blame them? 'Member how we felt when we first came?" chuckled Vi.

"Sort of exalted and plumb scared to death," interpreted Billie. "Those were the days of big fun, though."

"And the big fights," giggled Laura. "Remember how Amanda Peabody and that shadow of hers, Eliza Dilks, used to ride us to death?"

"Where do you get that stuff—used to?" demanded Vi slangily. "Why, I'll tell you something. Just this morning Amanda tried to pick a quarrel with me."

"Over what?" Billie was interested. Amanda Peabody was one of the most unpleasant girls at Three Towers Hall. She had money and had developed a sort of dashing good looks. Because of this some of the students—that smattering of toadies found among the girls of every boarding school—had rallied round her, forming a small, exclusive clique. Among the most conspicuous and faithful of Amanda's following was a girl named Eliza Dilks, otherwise known as "The Shadow."

"What did you and Amanda quarrel about?" Billie asked again.

"I didn't quarrel about anything," returned Vi virtuously. "It was Amanda who did the quarreling, and it was all about some silly little thing like a pencil that she accused me of taking from her desk in the study hall. Of course it was all nonsense. Why should I want her pencil when I have that beautiful silver one Uncle Dan gave me for Christmas?"

"What did you tell her?" Laura wanted to know.

"What would I tell her? I merely went by with my nose in the air and refused to answer her. She looked mad enough to bite nails," with a reminiscent giggle.

Laura sighed.

"I suppose that girl will be a thorn in our side——"

"Flesh," corrected Billie with a giggle.

"I said 'side' and I meant it," retorted Laura firmly. "Anyway, I suppose neither you nor Vi will deny that Amanda Peabody and Eliza Dilks are a thorny pair."

"Two thorns, without the roses," remarked Billie.

Vi began to chant in a soft, singsong:

"Oh, Amanda and her Shadow,

Amanda and her crony,

Went out to take the air one day,

Aridin' on a pony.

They thought they were the bees' headlight,

They thought they looked so tony.

But everyone they met called out,

'Go home! Your style is phony!'"

Billie and Laura applauded dutifully and Billie demanded to know how long Vi had been keeping this unsuspected talent a secret from her chums.

"You look romantic enough, Vi, goodness knows, but we never suspected you of being a poetess."

"Then don't now," urged Vi. "I wouldn't be guilty of such 'poetry.' It's Connie's."

"She should be shot at daybreak," remarked Laura. "I'll see to it myself."

"Oh, I don't know. It's a pretty good 'pome,'" chuckled Billie. "I've a notion to put it to music and adopt it as the new school song. Where is Connie, anyway? I thought she was coming with us for a hike?"

"She had to rewrite that composition on hitchhikers. Miss Johnson,"—a teacher of English at Three Towers Hall—"said it was too flippant." Laura finished with a chuckle, for Connie had read that composition to Billie and her chums the evening before, sitting cross-legged, like a young Chinese idol, on Billie's bed. It had been flippant—like Connie—and full of fun. The girls had laughed uproariously.

"Miss Johnson is dried up and old, a hopeless spinster," was Vi's merciless indictment of the English teacher. "She can't be expected to recognize honest fun when she sees it."

"Shouldn't be surprised but what Connie's second theme would be more flippant than her first," giggled Laura. "Then what will poor Miss Johnson do?"

"In that case, I certainly feel sorry for Connie," laughed Billie.

"Oh, I don't know. Maybe Miss Johnson would fall over in a fit and never come fully out of it. Then we'd all be freed from her. Me, I wish she would," declared Vi a bit vindictively.

The girls came out on the high promontory overlooking the lake, and halted in mute appreciation of the lovely view spread out before them. They had seen it many times before, but the fresh sight of it never failed to thrill them.

Boxton Military Academy stood high and proud on the crest of a hill, its parades and drill grounds marked out in patches of green velvet. From where they stood the girls could hear the beating of a drum and the fanfare of spirited music.

"No wonder the boys love it there," murmured Laura. "We should have a band at Three Towers. Might liven things up a bit."

"That would be lovely," laughed Vi. "I speak to play the big drum and you can take the bass horn, Laura. Billie, what's your choice? I suggest the trombone."

Billie chuckled.

"I'll speak to Miss Walters about it as soon as we get back," she promised. "Meanwhile, get busy, lazybones, and garner some of this goldenrod."

The yellow flame of the gorgeous weed covered the top of the promontory so that the girls were confronted by an embarrassment of riches. In a few moments their arms were filled with the golden blossoms.

"Aren't they the loveliest things you ever saw, girls?" cried Billie.

"Yes, they are. I adore this bright yellow, whether it's in flowers or dresses or hangings. It always makes me feel more cheerful."

"I wonder how anyone can have a favorite flower. It always seems to me that the flower I'm looking at at the moment is my favorite. Just now, of course, it's goldenrod. To-morrow it may be roses, for instance."

"Come on, let's start back," said Vi.

Laura and Vi had turned to go back when a sharp cry from Billie startled them. When they looked in the direction whence the cry had come, Billie Bradley was nowhere to be seen!

CHAPTER II
A DESPERATE FIX

LAURA and Vi dashed through the field of goldenrod to the spot where they had last seen Billie Bradley. They called to her and received a faint answer from somewhere far below.

"She's gone over the cliff!" gasped Vi.

"There are rocks down there, too," muttered Laura. She parted the bushes and peered below. "Billie, Billie! Where are you?"

A voice responded gallantly, battling with fear:

"I'm down here. My dress is caught on something. I daren't move, for fear it will tear. If you could reach me a stick or a rope, or something———"

"Sounds easy!" Laura sprang to her feet and looked wildly about her. "But where are we going to find the stick or the rope long enough to reach—Vi, what have you got?"

Vi had dashed through the field of goldenrod to a wooded patch in the background. Now she returned, bearing a long, forked stick.

"Looks like an uprooted tree," gasped Laura hysterically.

"So it is, I guess. If it's only long enough to reach Billie!"

The two girls flung themselves face downward on the edge of the cliff. They were almost afraid to part the bushes and look below for fear Billie had already disappeared.

She was still there, clinging desperately to the rocky, moss-covered face of the cliff. One hand clutched a runner of tough vine, the other clawed helplessly at loose dirt. Her feet could find no hold whatever, but dangled, impotent and useless, over the glazed surface of a huge, flat rock.

The thing that had saved her from being dashed upon the pointed rocks at the foot of the cliff was the clump of dwarfed bushes growing between the rocks in which her stout linen dress had caught and held. The dress still held. But if it gave way, or if the clump of bushes should come loose from the rocks, what would happen to Billie Bradley?

This agonized thought found an echo in the hearts of Laura Jordon and Vi Farrington as they lay there on the edge of the cliff, staring downward.

Laura impatiently caught the long stick from Vi's trembling hand.

"I'm stronger than you are. Let me try!"

At the spot where the two girls lay, Billie was almost directly beneath them. If the stick proved long enough, it would be an easy matter for her to grasp it with her one free hand. If it proved long enough——

Laura lowered the stick over the side of the cliff, hoping, praying, that it would reach Billie's groping hand.

There! It was extended to the utmost and still came a good two feet short of the imperiled girl.

"Vi, hold my feet!" commanded Laura. "Hold me so I can't go over myself. I'm going to try once more."

With Vi clinging to her feet, Laura wriggled further over the edge of the cliff. Having progressed as far as she could and being herself in imminent danger of losing her balance and plunging head downward upon those sharp-pointed rocks, Laura clung there, stretching her muscles until they ached, striving to bring the stick within the grasp of Billie's groping fingers.

The stick would not reach. Billie still hung there, at the mercy of the stout material in her dress, which might give way at any moment. What were they to do?

While the girls are striving desperately to find an answer to this question, a moment will be taken to introduce Billie Bradley and her chums to those who have not already made their acquaintance.

The three girls had been chums since those good old days when Billie Bradley had inherited the queer old house at Cherry Corners, as related in the first volume of this series, entitled, "Billie Bradley and Her Inheritance." In the attic of the queer old house Billie and her chums had discovered a small fortune in rare old postage stamps and coins.

This lucky discovery later proved the open sesame to Three Towers Hall, the boarding school toward which Billie had long turned yearning, but none-too-hopeful, eyes.

Life at Three Towers had exceeded even Billie's happy expectations. To be sure, there had been a few heartaches, a few defeats, but these were more than offset by the many victories, the many friends that Billie won for herself in her new environment. Laura Jordon and Violet Farrington, long friends and admirers of Billie Bradley, found their friendship cemented into a firm bond by the mutually shared experiences at Three Towers Hall.

Later, Billie and her chums spent an exciting and decidedly worthwhile summer at Lighthouse Island as the guests of Connie Danvers, whose father owned a summer bungalow there.

Back at Three Towers Hall again, the girls found themselves in the midst of a mystery, the solution of which brought undreamed-of happiness to a widow and her three children.

There had been other vacations which the chums had shared, prominent among them being that interesting and exciting summer spent at Twin Lakes. Another, more recent adventure was that which befell them at Treasure Cove where the three girls and their friends unearthed an old sea chest filled with rare silks, carved ivory, coins, and precious gems.

In the volume directly preceding this, entitled, "Billie Bradley at Sun Dial Lodge," Billie and her chums met with a series of alarming but fascinating adventures which finally led to the solution of an astonishing mystery.

Billie, who had been christened Beatrice but was seldom called by the more formal name, was a dark-haired, dark-eyed, energetic young person, whose overflowing vitality constantly demanded action. She was the undoubted leader of her small group and it was a tribute to Billie's personality that her friends not only deferred to her, but liked doing it.

Billie's family was small, but suited her exactly. Martin Bradley, her father, was a real estate and insurance broker, at which he was moderately successful. Mrs. Bradley was a charming woman, loved by her friends and adored by her family. There was a son, Billie's brother, Chetwood, commonly known as Chet. Between this brother and sister was a genuine regard and a similarity of tastes, a foundation for the best kind of comradeship.

Perhaps Billie's very best chum was Laura Jordon. Laura was fair-haired and blue-eyed and somewhat spoiled by being able to do as she liked about almost everything. Teddy Jordon was fair-haired and blue-eyed like his sister, a fine lad who was popular with boys and girls alike. Raymond Jordon, the father of the likable pair, owned a controlling interest in the big jewelry factory at North Bend, thus providing his offspring with a bit more spending money than was strictly good for them.

Violet Farrington, another very good chum of Billie's, was an only child but a very happy one, blessed with a pair of doting parents who made up to her whatever lack the girl might otherwise have felt in her brotherless and sisterless state.

Beside Chet Bradley and Teddy Jordon, there was a third lad often found in the company of Billie and her chums. His name was Ferd Stowing. Ferd was a likable, easy-going young fellow with a commendable knack for making other people comfortable.

These three boys attended Boxton Military Academy, the school for boys on Lake Molata, directly across from Three Towers Hall. When at home the sextette of young people lived at North Bend, a thriving town of some twenty thousand inhabitants. Forty miles of railroad travel transported one from the heart of North Bend to the heart of New York City. It was a pleasant place to live, as the boys and girls agreed.

During their activities in and about North Bend and at Three Towers Hall, the girls had encountered many adventures, some thrilling, some sad, but all more or less spiced with danger. None, however, had found them in such desperate fix as the one in which they were now involved.

Billie hung over that precipitous drop to the rocks at the base of the cliff with only the stout cloth of her dress between her and almost certain death.

It was impossible to get her from above. The ground sloped abruptly and it was covered by flat rocks and moss so that it would be impossible to gain a foothold.

Laura sprang to her feet and looked about her desperately.

"If we could only reach her from below, Vi! There's just a chance we might be able to climb up to her——"

"There is a path to the lake," said Vi, her teeth chattering with excitement. "But it's all around Robin Hood's barn. We haven't time——"

A faint cry reached them, tinged with desperation.

"Girls, do hurry! I can't cling here much longer! The cloth is beginning to—tear!"

CHAPTER III
EDINA TO THE RESCUE

At Billie Bradley's desperate cry, Laura flung herself at the edge of the cliff.

"I'm coming, Billie!" she shouted. "I'll get to you some way, if I break my own neck."

Vi caught her and dragged her back.

"Wait!" she cried. "Someone is down there near the lake!"

Laura looked where Vi pointed and saw a small figure at the foot of the cliff. It looked terribly far off, standing there on the massed rocks bordering the lake. Moreover, judging from the clothes she wore, the stranger was only a girl like themselves. Laura and Vi felt that it would take a man's strength to rescue Billie from her fearful predicament.

The girl made a megaphone of her hands and shouted up to Billie.

"Hold fast a minute! I'll get up to you!"

Laura and Vi watched, fascinated, as the girl began to ascend the steep face of the cliff hand over hand like a monkey. She made amazingly swift progress; but each moment the onlooking girls expected, feared, that she would lose her grip, go hurtling over backward to a horrible fate on the sharp-pointed, massed rocks at the foot of the cliff.

Meanwhile, Billie Bradley was striving to keep up heart and courage as she pressed her body close against the rock of the cliff face, clinging to the stout vine with nerveless fingers, striving to find a foothold for her dangling feet.

Each time she moved, a wave of fear swept over her as the stout linen cloth of her frock threatened to give way. She dared not even try to help herself, for fear that one support would fail her!

Then the dress began to give beneath her weight, as she hung there, dangling over eternity. She heard the sibilant hiss of splitting cloth and braced herself for whatever fate might be in store for her.

It was then that she became aware that someone was approaching from below. At first she thought that it was either Laura or Vi and wondered how it was possible for them to have made their way around to the foot of the cliff in such a short time.

However, in another moment or two, the girl came within her range of vision and she saw that the newcomer was neither Laura nor Vi, but a person who was a stranger to her.

Another rip of tearing cloth sent a shudder through Billie. The stranger made amazingly swift progress up that dangerous ascent, but Billie knew she must come very quickly if she was going to be in time. Another few moments, and the rescuer would have arrived—too late!

Another ripping and tearing sound, and Billie's weight sagged. She clung desperately, with numbing fingers, to that clump of stout vine. She knew by the feel of it in her hand that it was breaking loose. In another minute or two the roots would be dislodged.

"Oh, hurry!" she called to the strange, gallant girl, who continued her steady upward progress. "I've only a few moments left——"

"Hold fast! Never give up the ship! I'll git up to that there shelf if it takes a leg!"

The stranger was gasping from her exertions but her voice was round and hearty, full of a vitality that Billie found tremendously reassuring.

The strange girl rapidly closed the distance between herself and Billie. She climbed to a narrow ledge of rock that had been invisible to Billie from where she hung and, across the space of three or four feet, the eyes of the two girls met and clung.

Then Billie turned her eyes away. What could the strange girl do, now that she was so near? She was in almost as precarious a position as Billie herself, and certainly she had nothing at hand with which to help except her own unaided hands and strength.

Suddenly Billie gasped and groped frantically at the cliff face. The clump of vine had come loose in her hands, the sound of rending cloth told her that the stout threads of her dress had parted at last! With wild panic at her heart, she felt herself falling!

Something slapped the cliff face close to her clawing hand. A voice said sharply:

"Grab that! Quick!"

Instinctively, Billie grabbed, clung.

The authoritative voice cried again:

"Now then! Help yourself if you can. This ledge makes purty good footin', though slippery. Hang on now. I'll pull you up!"

Billie clung to the leather belt flung her by the strange girl. In the interstices of the rock she managed to gain a toehold, and by a prodigious effort and with the help of the strange girl she managed to draw herself up to the ledge. There she clung, while an overpowering dizziness assailed her. She swayed weakly, feeling faint and dizzy, half expecting to plunge over the narrow ledge, but past caring very much whether she did or not.

A sharp, angry voice broke through her failing consciousness.

"Not going to faint on me, are you? After me taking all the trouble to save your life? Say! You make me good and tired!"

No shock of icy water could have reacted upon Billie Bradley with better effect. She made a desperate effort to collect her failing senses. She opened her eyes and stared vaguely at the hard young face thrust so close to her own. She was dimly aware that an equally hard, strong young arm had been thrust behind her shoulders, pressing her close to the face of the cliff.

"Well, are you a quitter or ain't you?" the rude voice demanded. "I can't get you down there all by myself. Chances are, if you faint, we'll both go crashing down onto them pointed rocks. And they won't make a soft bed, I promise you! Well, how about it? Are you going to faint—or ain't you?"

By a supreme effort Billie regained control of her slipping senses. She stared coldly at the round, hard face of the young stranger.

"I'm not a quitter," she said. "And I assure you, I have no intention of fainting." After a moment she added, as though as an afterthought: "Thank you for saving my life!"

The strange girl grinned.

"Don't mention it! Only I ain't saved it yet. Reckon both of us have got to look sharp if we want to get out of this jam alive. It ain't no easy going down this hill, let me tell you! Now then! Ready?"

Bitterly ashamed of her recent weakness, Billie assented. She would have died rather than admit, even to herself, that her head was still whirling and that she was forced to clench her teeth to keep them from chattering.

That descent to the jagged rocks at the base of the cliff was one long nightmare. If it had not been for the help and encouragement of the strange girl, interspersed with occasional merciless taunts from the same source, Billie knew she could never have made it.

As it was, she slipped and half fell, half slid the last fifteen or twenty feet, finally landing amid a shower of pebbles and dirt in a crevasse between two jagged rocks.

"Mercy!" she gasped.

"It is a mercy that you landed betwixt instead of on 'em."

Billie looked up from her undignified position to find the strange girl grinning down at her. She frowned and tried to rise, but found herself wedged in so tightly that she could scarcely move.

"Like a sardine in a packed can," remarked the strange girl unkindly.

Billie wanted to feel offended, but she could not. The comparison was too apt. She met the quizzical, smiling glance of the strange girl and suddenly laughed.

"You are a very frank person. But I do feel rather like a sardine. If you will give me a hand, I think I can manage, if I try hard enough, to get out of this ridiculous place."

The pulling and tugging that ensued was a painful process for Billie. She discovered that there was scarcely a portion of her body that failed to boast either bruise or scratch.

"I'm pretty well disabled," she admitted. "No tennis and no rowing for me for a few days to come at least."

"'Twouldn't be best to try, I guess," remarked the girl.

Ruefully, Billie bent to examine her torn skirt. As she straightened up, a sharp exclamation escaped her.

"Hold on there! Where are you going?"

CHAPTER IV
BATTLE

EVEN as Billie Bradley spoke, the strange girl disappeared into the woods.

"Please don't go! Please! You mustn't until I've had a chance to thank you!"

At the urgent request, or command, the girl reappeared, but with obvious reluctance. She stood awkwardly, rubbing one foot over the other.

"Don't want any thanks," she muttered. "Didn't do nothing, nohow. I guess—I guess—I'd better go now."

Billie was nonplused by the strange behavior of this young person who had just saved her life. The manner of the girl had altered completely. From being dictatorial, "bossy," and almost offensively sure of herself, she had become a shy and awkward country girl. Her eyes avoided Billie's direct look, whether from shyness or sullenness, it was impossible to tell.

Billie, painfully conscious of all her cuts and bruises, went up to the girl and held out her hand.

"Whether you like it or not, I'm going to thank you. My life doesn't mean a lot to you probably," with a whimsical smile, "but it does to me and I am very properly grateful for it. How you can climb!" she added with genuine admiration. "If I could scale the side of a cliff like that, I wouldn't care whether I could solve a problem in algebra or not."

The girl flashed Billie a glance. There was both sullenness and shyness in it; which was odd, considering the dictatorial tone she had used to Billie a few moments earlier.

"Don't be so nice to me," she said, in a hard voice, "until you know who I am!"

Billie was given no opportunity to comment on this peculiar observation for at the moment Vi and Laura dashed in from the woods, rushed to Billie and flung their arms about her. They had come by the woods path "around Robin Hood's barn" and had reached her as soon as possible.

"Oh-h, look out! Don't hug so tightly, darlings. I'm—to put it mildly—sensitive. Yes, I'm alive—as you see. No there are no bones broken—I think. But I'll have to soak in arnica to-night. Bruises—hundreds of 'em. But I'm not complaining. I know how lucky I am just to be alive!"

Animated by the same thought, Laura and Vi left off hugging Billie and turned to the strange girl.

"We don't know how to thank you," Vi began.

"If you knew how much I hate thanks you wouldn't go to the bother," responded the stranger ungraciously. "I don't do such things for thanks. Well—good-by!" She turned abruptly and would have plunged into the woods had not Billie called her.

"I don't know why you have taken such a sudden dislike to me—to us," she said. "I am sorry if I have done or said anything to offend you. After saving my life, I don't like you to go away angry."

"I'm not mad," muttered the girl. "And I don't dislike you. I think you're grand!"

Was ever such a contradictory, amazing creature? Billie stared at her in helpless bewilderment.

"Well, then!"

The girl suddenly flung up her head. Her round face was stern and her mouth was combative, but there were tears in her eyes!

"You won't be so nice to me when you know who I am, I tell you," she blurted. "You'll be like all the rest of the sneerin', titterin' lot of 'em. I hate them, I hate every last one of them!"

This outburst amazed the three girls and roused their curiosity. What did the strange creature mean?

"It's true I don't know your name or where you come from," said Billie. "But I am sure I shall like you just as much and be just as grateful to you for having saved my life, whoever you are."

"Well, then, my name is Edina Tooker," the girl threw out the information like a challenge. "And I'm livin', just at present, at Three Towers Hall!"

The girls merely stared at her, doubting if they had heard aright. The self-styled Edina Tooker laughed harshly.

"You see! A crazy lookin' jay like me couldn't be goin' to your select boarding school, could she? That's what you're thinking, isn't it? Oh, you don't need to answer me! I can see it in your faces!"

There was a world of bitterness behind the girl's harsh tone.

"She has been hurt," thought Billie. "Pretty badly hurt and her pride is up in arms."

Before she could speak Laura said impulsively:

"Why, you can't be a student at Three Towers Hall. I've never even seen you there!"

"I only come a few days ago," the girl explained. "And after the first day I—I kep' close to my own room."

That explained it, thought Billie. She had heard of the new girl from the wild open spaces who dressed like a freak, talked worse, and kept to her dormitory as though it were a burrow from which she seldom emerged except to attend classes. Characteristically, these uncomplimentary rumors had come to her through Amanda Peabody. Billie had intended vaguely to look up the new girl to see if she could be of any help. Instead, the new girl had looked her up—and in a most dramatic fashion!

"I know who you are," Billie said, friendly eyes on the sullen face of Edina Tooker. "I'm glad you introduced yourself. I was going to look you up, anyway."

The sullen expression on Edina Tooker's face did not lift. She regarded Billie suspiciously.

"What for?" she demanded. "So you could see what a freak I am and laugh at me behind my back?"

This accusation was almost too much for even Billie's good nature. A sharp retort rose to her lips—but got no further. She realized in time how much this strange girl must have suffered to make her so bitter and resentful. She was showing tooth and claw because that was her only method of defense. Like some wild creature of the woods, she was backed up against a wall, unable to distinguish friend from foe, fighting valiantly and indiscriminately, fearing nothing but surrender.

Billie, holding a firm check upon her temper, replied gently:

"My main—in fact, my only idea in deciding to look you up was to see if I could help you."

"Why should you think I needed help?" retorted Edina Tooker harshly. "I suppose you'd been hearin' things about me—what a freak I am and all."

"No one ever said you were a freak," Billie pursued patiently. "But you were a new girl from a distant city and I thought you might be glad to have someone sort of—well, show you the ropes."

The corners of Edina's straight young mouth turned downward in a sneer.

"Sounds good, the way you tell it. But you can't fool me. You're all alike up to that school, with your highfallutin' manners and uppity ways. You'd come to see me, yes, so that you could laugh at me and talk about me afterward. 'Native,' 'barbarian,' that's a couple o' the names I've heard your swell friends call me. Mebbe you could add some to the string."

"If Billie can't, I will!" cried Laura, with sudden fury. "You're nothing but a heathen and an ungrateful wretch! You don't know who Billie Bradley is, maybe, but I'll teach you!"

"Hush, Laura, please! Come away!"

Laura would not be silenced. She brushed the interruption aside impatiently and rushed on, her words pouring forth in a torrent:

"Billie Bradley is the most popular girl at Three Towers Hall. She does almost everything better than anybody else and yet the girls love her just the same. Maybe you've got sense enough to know what that means. She's a perfect peach and any girl she takes up may count herself in luck. You just think of that when you are all alone and try to realize what you've lost. Come on Billie, let's get away from here!"

Laura turned away with one last, inimical look at Edina Tooker. Vi joined her, but Billie still lingered behind.

"I'm sorry you feel this way," she said to the girl who had saved her life. "I owe you a debt and I'd like to be friends." Billie paused but as Edina remained silent with sullenly averted face, Billie went on to join Laura and Vi.

She did not know that the strange girl looked after her with eyes suddenly blurred by tears.

CHAPTER V
A PUBLIC REBUKE

Laura Jordon's resentment against Edina Tooker and her attitude toward Billie did not abate at once. For the greater part of the return walk to Three Towers Hall she sputtered and fumed, mentioning dire forms of punishment that should be meted out to the girl from the West if she, Laura, could have her way.

"Never saw such an ungrateful wretch in my life. Talk about throwing pearls before swine! She never even knew what it meant to be taken up by Billie Bradley."

"I doubt if she knows now." Billie paused and said "ouch" as a stretched ligament protested sharply.

"Well, she will before she has been at Three Towers much longer," prophesied Vi. "Personally, I can't bear the girl and I hope she gets everything that's coming to her."

Billie frowned, partly with pain at her cuts and bruises, partly in disapproval of Vi's uncompromising attitude.

"I'm sure I can't feel that way about her. The girl saved my life and I owe her something for that."

"So do we," said Laura promptly. "But did you notice how she flung my thanks back in my face?"

"Appears to be a habit with her," remarked Vi flippantly.

"It looks to me as though the girl had been hurt past bearing by the persecution and ridicule of some of the girls at the Hall. She has pride and spirit and is ready to strike out at everybody."

"It seems to me I detect Amanda Peabody's fine hand in this," observed Laura. "Amanda would enjoy nothing better than a cat-and-mouse game with a girl like Edina Tooker."

"She seems to be poor——"

"I've heard differently," said Billie. "One of the girls told me her father was getting rich fast—struck oil on an Oklahoma ranch, or something of the sort."

"Well, she may be rich; but, if she looks it, I'm an Indian," returned Laura skeptically. "Never saw a girl dressed like that who was anything but poverty-stricken."

"She probably hasn't the slightest idea how to dress," observed Billie. "I can imagine Edina Tooker in riding breeches or middy and skirt doing a movie on some rocky mountain trail. In that sort of setting she would be very much a part of the picture. But transplant her to a fashionable girls' school and she—well, she just doesn't fit."

"A round peg in a very square hole," observed Vi.

"Exactly. I feel sorry for the poor girl. She's in for a hard time."

Toward the end of the tramp back to Three Towers, Billie found herself becoming very weary. She paused often to rest and was finally forced to accept the help of her chums. An arm about the shoulders of each of the girls, she hobbled on, acutely conscious of all her cuts and bruises and the strained and aching ligaments in her arms and legs.

They were on the last steep slope that ended at the boathouse in front of the Hall when they heard the deep-toned gong that announced supper in the dining hall.

Billie cried out in alarm and tried to hobble on more swiftly.

"I'll make you girls late and Debsy has charge of the dining hall this week." "Debsy" was the nickname for Miss Debbs, teacher of elocution. "You know what that means!"

"One whole afternoon of imprisonment in the dorm and a discredit mark besides," Vi interpreted. "Debsy sure is death on tardiness."

"You girls go ahead and leave me," Billie begged. "You can make it even now if you run. I'll get along all right."

"Never!" said Laura dramatically. "I am with you to the death!"

"Don't be silly!" cried Billie. "Please go on, girls. It won't do me a bit of good for you all to get into trouble."

"We will never leave you until death—or Debsy—do us part," chuckled Vi. "You'd better save your breath, Billie. You will need it for this last wild dash up the hill."

By the time they reached the Hall Billie was painfully out of breath and aching in every muscle.

"You go on—in," she gasped. "I've got to—wash up a little—and change my dress. I'm a sight."

"We'll help you," decided Laura.

Despite Billie's protests, her two chums rushed her up the stairs to the dormitory. There Vi ran water into a bowl while Laura invaded the closet to get down a fresh frock.

"There! Stick your head in that, Billie. You do have a look of battle and sudden death about you. And your hair could stand a comb. So! Much, much better. Now you bear a slight resemblance to the Billie Bradley I have known and loved so faithfully."

Over Billie's freshened head Laura slipped a cool, peach-colored frock; then ran to the lavatory to wash her own hands. This service Vi also performed for herself. In less time than they had thought possible, the chums were ready to face the eagle eye of the dreaded Miss Debbs.

They made their way decorously to the dining hall, entered as unobtrusively as possible, and slipped quietly to their seats.

In spite of all their precautions, their entrance was observed by practically everybody in the room. Friends of the chums, who were in the majority, pretended not to see them. Their few enemies, led by Amanda Peabody and her shadow, Eliza Dilks, stared openly and tittered.

Billie did not raise her eyes from her plate as Connie Danvers, seated beside her, passed the cold meat and salad.

"Fill up your plate, quick," whispered Connie. "Maybe Debsy didn't notice you."

"Such a chance!" returned Billie, scarcely moving her lips. "I can feel her eagle eye on me now!"

Through the steady murmur of voices and the clatter of plates and cutlery broke the deep, husky voice of the redoubtable Miss Debbs.

"Beatrice Bradley! Stand, if you please!"

Billie shot a sidelong glance at Connie Danvers.

"I'm in for it now!" she whispered, and got to her feet.

"Yes, Miss Debbs," she said politely.

"You are aware that there is a strict rule against tardiness—especially at meals—are you not?" Miss Debbs could ask the simplest question in an highly histrionic manner, as though the weight of worlds depended on the answer.

Now Billie answered meekly:

"Yes, Miss Debbs."

"Yet you deliberately enter this hall at five minutes past the hour?"

Billie raised her eyes to meet the boring glance of the elocution teacher.

"Not deliberately, Miss Debbs. We—I had an accident."

Miss Debbs brushed the excuse aside with a dramatic sweep of the hand.

"Nevertheless, you admit that you were late?"

Billie could scarcely hope to deny it in the face of all the evidence against her. Nevertheless, she repeated, meekly:

"Yes, Miss Debbs."

"You will report to me promptly at ten o'clock to-morrow morning."

With another queenly gesture Miss Debbs pantomimed permission for Billie to be seated, of which tacit permission Billie immediately availed herself.

Connie Danvers whispered viciously:

"It isn't fair! Laura and Vi were just as late as you."

"Debsy doesn't like me," whispered Billie, and her eyes twinkled. "She never has since the day I refused to use my hands when I recited 'Lochinvar.' I never could fling my hands about as she does. I'd feel a perfect fool."

"She'll give you a discredit, sure," worried Connie. "And you can't afford too many, Billie, or you'll be barred from tennis and rowing."

The words merely echoed the worry in Billie's heart. To be barred from her beloved athletics was tragedy too dire to be considered. She knew, too, that a discredit beside her name so early in the term was enough to start her off "on the wrong foot."

While she was considering the advisability of taking the matter to Miss Walters, the wise and well-loved head of Three Towers Hall, she glanced up and met the gloating eyes of Amanda Peabody.

"You think you're smart," the look seemed to say. "Yet here you are in bad at the very beginning of the term."

Amanda bent over and whispered something to Eliza Dilks. The two girls tittered and glanced sneeringly at Billie. Their enjoyment of her predicament was obvious, yet Billie continued to eat roast beef and the very excellent salad without appearing disconcerted in the least. It was this ability of hers to disguise her feelings that often infuriated Amanda and her toadying shadow to the point of open and indiscreet betrayal of their enmity toward Billie and her chums.

One such occasion was this one. Amanda bent across the table toward Billie and said in a voice that was audible to every one:

"Dare you to tell where you went this afternoon!"

The gabble of voices settled into a momentary hush as the other girls regarded these ancient antagonists.

Billie looked up and met the sneering gaze of Amanda Peabody with a smile.

"I've not the slightest objection," she answered calmly. "We went to gather goldenrod."

"Goldenrod!" ejaculated Amanda, with a titter. "That's a good one!"

"You might ask her where it is," and Eliza Dilks nudged her crony with an oversharp elbow.

"Where what is?" asked Billie.

"The goldenrod. How much did you bring back with you?"

Before Billie could reply there came a disturbance at the door. Innumerable pairs of bright, curious eyes were turned upon the fantastic figure in the doorway.

Billie recognized the newcomer. It was Edina Tooker.

CHAPTER VI
BILLIE IS LOYAL

EDINA TOOKER faced the battery of curious, amused glances like a thoroughbred. Even when a ripple of laughter ruffled the serene atmosphere of the room, she did not flinch nor cower. If anything, her back was held more stiffly erect, her head was flung back with a defiant gesture. Billie was reminded of an unbroken colt who feels the flick of the whip for the first time and is hurt and enraged by the pain even while he fails to understand the reason for his punishment.

Billie was seized by an almost irresistible desire to go and range herself at this girl's side, to beat down the ridicule that surged toward the defenseless stranger in a merciless tide.

Edina Tooker wore a heavily pleated serge skirt, far too wide and too long to meet the demands of the prevailing fashion. Over this, accentuating her naturally bulky proportions, was a stiffly starched white shirtwaist, adorned by a flowing red tie.

Her hair was naturally very thick and of that peculiar black which seems to hide a bluish tinge in its depths; but it was drawn back ruthlessly from her broad brow and round red face, drawn back so harshly that it pulled her heavy straight brows upward, giving an odd, almost diabolical, expression to her face.

She wore "sensible" stockings that were very thick and durable and that served admirably to disguise the natural shapeliness of her limbs. On her feet were not shoes, but heavy boots that laced half-way up to her knees!

Even Billie, sensible as she was to this strange girl's suffering, resentful as she was of her friends' amusement, knew Edina Tooker to be a figure of fun as she stood there in that assemblage of carefully cared for, tastefully yet simply dressed young people.

"Why doesn't she sit down?" thought Billie, in exasperation. "Why does she stand there and take the limelight? It's idiotic!"

The ripple of amusement continuing, Miss Debbs looked up from absorption in her meal and met the defiant gaze of Edina Tooker. Miss Debbs' face grew red.

"Another tardy one!" she exclaimed. "What do you mean, Edina Tooker, by reporting here at this late hour?"

The girl's face grew sullen. She scraped one clumsy boot over the other.

"I couldn't help it, Miss Debbs," she said, in a voice scarcely audible. "I just come back."

"Came," corrected Miss Debbs in her deep, husky voice. "Try to speak grammatical English, at least! May I ask," she added sarcastically, "where you have been and why you have just come back?"

The ripple of amusement rose again, surging toward the girl in the outlandish garb. Edina's face was scarlet, her lip trembled in spite of a gallant effort at self-control.

"I—I went for a walk," she said.

"Ah!" declaimed Miss Debbs in her best elocutionary style. "You went for a walk! May I ask where you went for a walk at this time of the evening, neglecting to return to Three Towers Hall until ten minutes past the supper hour?"

Edina shifted from one foot to the other. Her scarlet face was pitiful to see. She tried to speak, but was apparently unable to bring forth a sound.

Billie Bradley could bear it no longer. She got to her feet and faced the teacher.

"If you please, Miss Debbs, I can tell you where Edina Tooker has been and why she was late for the supper hour!"

Here was drama! There was the sound of a concerted gasp as all eyes swerved to Billie. Edina Tooker put up a trembling hand to her shining black hair and also gazed at Billie.

Miss Debbs looked outraged, but interested.

"What do you mean, Beatrice Bradley? Explain!" she commanded.

Without hesitation, Billie told in a low, clear voice of the trip up to Goldenrod Point, as it was called by the students of Three Towers, of her fall over the cliff, a fall which had almost had disastrous consequences, of Edina Tooker's brave and efficient help in a moment of extreme peril, and of her own eventual return to safety.

She ended boldly, carried away by her own eloquence:

"I think, instead of a discredit mark, Edina Tooker deserves a medal for heroism. I know if I had *my* way she should have it!"

Billie made a gesture toward the door and paused, feeling rather foolish. Edina Tooker had disappeared!

Many pairs of eyes followed Billie's glance toward the door and a babble of excited voices arose.

"Where has she gone?"

"What did she have to do that for?"

"Just when we were all getting ready to give her three cheers——"

"*And* a tiger!"

Through the commotion broke the voice of Miss Debbs.

"Silence, please! You will resume your seats and your supper. You will act, if you please, as though nothing had happened. While I am in charge this confusion must cease. Silence!"

When order had been partially restored, Miss Debbs turned her attention to Billie.

"I am obliged to you for your defense of this extraordinary girl. One wonders whether, if you had not spoken up for her, she would have said a word in her own behalf."

"I doubt it, Miss Debbs," said Billie earnestly. "She's the sort who hates thanks and I think I embarrassed her by speaking out."

"Unfortunately," resumed Miss Debbs, proceeding with her discourse as though Billie, by answering her query, had been guilty of an impertinence, "this girl has committed another indiscretion by leaving this room before she was given permission to do so. She appears lamentably ignorant of the rules by which Three Towers Hall is governed."

"I'll go and call her back, Miss Debbs." Billie rose eagerly in her place. "I don't think she can have got very far."

"Beatrice Bradley, you will stay where you are!" returned Miss Debbs severely. "You will not leave this room until I give you permission to do so."

Billie sank back in her seat with a sigh of resignation. Miss Debbs was being dramatic, and when she was in that mood there was no arguing with her. Billie did not try, but finished her meal with what appetite she could.

There was floating island for dessert and home-made chocolate cake, an ideal combination and a prime favorite with Billie. But she could not enjoy it for thinking of Edina wandering off somewhere by herself, Edina, heartsore and lonely and desperately rebellious.

The meal at an end, there was a general exodus of girls into the halls and spacious grounds of Three Towers Hall. There they were permitted to wander until nine o'clock when the melodious gong called them indoors to the dormitories and "lights out."

As usual, Billie Bradley found herself the center of a little court. About her gathered most of the worth-while girls of Three Towers Hall, students who had accomplished something in scholarship, in athletics, or both.

To-night she found herself more than ordinarily popular, because of the interest attached to her adventure of the afternoon and her contact with the girl who was already becoming a source of mystery and interested speculation to the students of Three Towers.

"You sure did champion that queer Edina Tooker, Billie," drawled Rose Belser. Rose was tall and dark and unusually good-looking. Once an enemy of Billie, Rose was now one of her warmest, most loyal friends. "I've never known you to be so eloquent."

"Even Debsy was impressed," giggled Connie Danvers. "I think it was rather a shock to her, Billie, to discover that you had so much dramatic talent."

"I was in earnest, and, you know, sincerity works wonders," laughed Billie. "Besides," more soberly, "I feel sorry for the girl. She doesn't fit here and she knows it."

"One wonders why she came," murmured Rachael Carew. Rachael, more commonly known as "Ray" Carew, was the only daughter of the wealthy Carews of Boston. While a thorough "good fellow" with those she considered her equals, Ray could be a bit of a snob with those whose social position was not secure. "One wonders still more," added Rachael, "how Miss Walters happened to admit a girl of that type to Three Towers Hall."

For some reason which she could not quite fathom herself, indignation blazed up in Billie at Rachael's patronizing tone.

"I don't know what you mean by 'that type of girl', Ray. She seems to me a thoroughly good sort——"

"A diamond in the rough?" drawled Ray.

"Perhaps," flashed Billie. "But I like her and she saved my life. I'd be worse than ungrateful if I consented to listen to unkind remarks about her."

Before the girls realized her intention or could make a move to stop her, Billie had pushed through the little group and started toward the broad, lighted portal of the Hall.

"The little spitfire!" murmured Rachael Carew. "Who would expect her to fly out at me like that? Anyone would think that queer jay of a girl was her twin sister, to hear her talk."

"You should know Billie well enough not to run down anyone who has done her a favor," Laura remarked. "Loyalty is Billie's dominating trait, you know."

"Of course it is," said Rose Belser. "That's why we all love her——"

"All except Amanda Peabody and Eliza Dilks," remarked Connie Danvers and began to sing softly under her breath:

Oh, Amanda and her Shadow,
Amanda and her crony,
Went out to take the air one day,
Ridin' on a pony."

A chorus of voices joined Connie in the second stanza of the verse:

They thought they were the bees' headlight,
They thought they looked so tony,
But every one they met called out,
Go home, your style is phony!'"

At the moment Amanda and Eliza and several of the younger girls passed close to the group and shot them a suspicious glance, which provoked a gale of mirth from the author of the "poem" and her friends.

"Let's sing it again, louder this time," proposed the irrepressible Connie, but Vi put a check on the hilarity.

"We have had plenty of trouble with those two girls and will probably have more in the future," she said. "There's no use going out of our way to look for it."

Meanwhile Billie had gone in search of Edina Tooker.

She was not in the first year dormitory. There were several girls gathered there, reading or studying, but they unanimously denied any knowledge as to Edina's whereabouts.

"She is probably mooning down by the lake somewhere," said one of them. "She likes to get away by herself."

Before continuing her search, Billie went down the back stairs to the roomy kitchen where the gastronomic needs of several scores of healthy girls were catered to each day.

There was a new cook, a huge black woman with skin like polished ebony and an expansive smile that showed two rows of glistening white teeth. The negress rejoiced in the name of Clarice and she was already one of Billie's devoted slaves.

"I need some sandwiches, Clarice, and a big piece of that delicious cake. I don't know," with calculated flattery, "when I have ever tasted such scrumptious cake. I ate so much at supper, it's only a wonder I'm not sick."

"Well, then, Miss Billie, Ah sho hopes as you don't git no tummyache tonight. An' Ah'm telling you they ain't much o' that cake left, but you's welcome to what I got, yes'm."

"You certainly are good to us, Clarice, as well as being a scrumptious cook," said the girl gratefully.

Five minutes later Billie crept out of a side door and made her way by a circuitous route down toward the lake. She carried a basket over her arm.

CHAPTER VII
A TALE OF RICHES

It was some time later that Billie Bradley was directed to the person she sought by the sound of heart-broken sobbing.

Silently, she made her way through the underbrush until she descried a figure in rumpled shirtwaist and pleated skirt, lying face downward on the thick grass.

"Please don't cry," said Billie. "And don't run away. I've brought you some supper."

At the sound of Billie Bradley's voice, Edina Tooker jumped to her feet and looked wildly about her. She dashed a hand across her eyes and then turned, as though about to dart off into the woods.

"Wait a minute!" cried Billie. "I've brought you some sandwiches and two luscious pieces of cake. If pressed," she added lightly, "I might consent to eat some with you."

As the girl paused and looked toward her, trying to pierce the darkness, Billie knew she had struck the right note. A friendly, offhand manner would win Edina Tooker more quickly than sympathy.

"Clarice has packed the basket to the top, bless her old black heart. We'll find a nice flat rock and regale ourselves to our hearts' content."

Billie found the rock without more delay and seated herself upon it, the basket between her knees.

After a moment of indecision Edina followed and flung herself full length on the ground beside Billie.

"Why did you come after me?" she queried listlessly. "You might better have left me alone."

The statement was not made ungraciously nor sullenly; it was merely as though the girl were unutterably weary and could not imagine anyone taking a legitimate interest in her or her affairs.

Billie said nothing, but handed out sandwiches and cake, which the girl accepted ravenously.

"I'm hungry," she said simply. "I haven't had a bite to eat since noon."

"You should have come in to supper," said Billie, nibbling at a piece of the matchless cake. "Debsy might have given you a bad mark for being late, but she couldn't have kept you from eating your supper."

"I didn't want any then. I couldn't go in and face those jeering, snickering girls." Edina Tooker clenched her hands and spoke with a sudden, desperate vehemence. "They think I'm a big joke and I—I hate them. I could kill them all!"

Billie waited patiently for the storm to pass. Then she said gently:

"Have a piece of cake, Edina. You've no idea how good it is."

"I don't want any cake," said Edina sullenly. She sat up, very stiff and straight, her hands locked about her humped knees. "I don't want anything. To-morrow I'm going back home."

Billie was startled.

"You are leaving Three Towers?"

Edina nodded unhappily.

"Three Towers has no use for me. I ain't ever been so unhappy in my life as I've been since I come—came—here. I never dreamed it would be like this."

"What did you think it would be like?" asked Billie gently.

"I don't know—exactly. But I thought people would be kind and I'd have a chance to git some book learnin' like I never had in my life. And I always wanted it, ever since I was old enough to ride my own cow pony. And now I—I gotta go home."

There was a choke in the quiet, sullen voice. Billie guessed what it would mean for Edina to return to the "cow country," carrying wounds that would never heal.

She said quietly:

"I wouldn't do that, if I were you, Edina. I wouldn't run away."

It was dark down there by the lake, but Billie could sense the quick motion of the girl's head as it turned toward her.

"You oughtn't to say that to me." After a while she added in a hopeless tone:

"Mebbe it would be runnin' away like you say, mebbe it would be quittin'. Jest the same," her voice rose passionately, "I'd ruther be horsewhipped than stand another week like the one I've just gone through!"

Billie waited a moment, then reached out and touched Edina's clenched fist where it rested on her voluminous skirt.

"Suppose you tell me something about yourself," she suggested. "I think I can help you. I want to. I owe you something, you know, for saving my life."

Edina hesitated for a moment; then began in a low, monotonous voice to tell the drab story of her life.

"Seems like we've always been poor, Paw and Maw and me," began Edina. "Ever since I was a little shaver, I can't remember anything but poverty. Paw was what you'd call a prospector."

"Gold?" asked Billie.

"No, oil. He had some property and he was always sure there was oil on it. Seems to me I can never remember the time he wasn't drillin' holes somewheres tryin' to strike a gusher.

"Maw and me we got fed up with it, what with bein' holed up in the same little neck of the woods all the time and never goin' nowheres nor havin' nothing. There were days we went hungry——"

The droning voice broke off suddenly and Billie had a startlingly clear vision of that tragic little family, dying of monotony, starving a good deal of the time, with nothing but a vision to sustain them.

"The worst of it was," the quiet voice continued, "that I never got much schoolin' and I always wanted it. I thought it would be heaven if the time ever come—came—when I could go to a real school like other girls and learn the sort of things that were put in books——

"It just goes to show," said Edina, after another pause, "that things ain't never the way you'd expect they'd be. When Paw struck oil——"

"He did?" ejaculated Billie.

"I thought me and Maw must be the happiest pair on earth. When Paw said I could come East and go to school here, I thought I'd die, I was that crazy with joy. And now here I am—and—and you see how it is. I can't hardly go back and face Maw, seems like."

Billie was thinking swiftly.

"If your father has struck oil on his property, he must be making a good deal of money, Edina."

"Guess so." The girl shrugged indifferently. "Paw said if the gusher kept on gushin' we'd probably be millionaires before we got through. But what good's it goin' to do me," hopelessly, "if I ain't even goin' to git an education out of it? I'm—goin' back home—to-morrow."

Billie came to a swift decision.

"You are going to do no such thing, Edina Tooker! You are going to stay right here at Three Towers Hall, and before long the girls will be begging your pardon for ever having dared to laugh at you!"

CHAPTER VIII
BILLIE AGAINST HER WORLD

THERE was a moment of silence broken only by the night sounds of the woods and the gentle lapping of the lake against the shore.

Then Edina Tooker drew a long, tremulous breath.

"It—sounds like—a fairy tale," she said huskily. "Seems like I'd have to change a lot to have that happen."

"So you will," said Billie Bradley eagerly. She was beginning to warm to her plan as it took form in her mind. "Not in yourself, you understand, but in, well, in externals—like clothes, for instance."

There! It was out! Even in the darkness Billie could guess at the hot flush that mantled the face of the girl from the West. As the silence continued and Edina sat with clenched hands, staring out toward the lake, Billie began to fear she had gone too far—that Edina's fierce pride would resent the insinuation in her friendly suggestion.

In a moment, however, Edina's quiet voice put her fears to rest.

"Everything about me's wrong. Don't you think I know that? All I need is eyes in my head to tell me I don't stack up against these girls here with their purty clothes and their airs and graces. We're a hundred—a thousand miles apart."

"Would you like to be like them, Edina—look like them, I mean?"

For the first time the girl showed animation.

"Oh, would I just!" she breathed. "Would I *just*! But I don't know how. I wouldn't know where to start."

"Well, *I* would," said Billie. "I'll guarantee to make you over into a perfect picture of the modern schoolgirl, Edina Tooker, as soon as—well, as soon as we can get a day off to do some shopping."

"Would you help me?" asked Edina, in a stifled tone. "*Would* you?"

"You'd be surprised," Billie retorted gaily. "I hope you have some sort of indelible identification mark on you, Edina Tooker. Otherwise, when I get through with you, you won't know yourself!"

There was no doubt but that the girl from Oklahoma, Billie's "rough diamond," was dazzled by the prospect.

"It don't seem hardly possible, but if you could fix me up like you say, I'd be grateful to you all the rest of my life."

"There's only one condition," said Billie severely; "and that is that you will agree to do exactly as I tell you, that you will let me have my own way about everything. It's the only way I can get results."

"Done!" cried Edina, and reached out a big rough hand that almost crushed Billie's little one in its grip. "You're sure a good sport and I'm sorry for the way I—I talked to you before."

"That's all right." Billie began to gather up the remnants of the basket lunch. "We'd best be getting back to the Hall or they will be sending out a posse in search of us. Besides, I promised Vi I'd help her with her math."

As the two girls approached the Hall, Edina walking close to Billie, her eyes downcast and sullen, they found that the school grounds were almost deserted.

The groups of girls had broken up and scattered indoors, most of them for study, some few of them for reading or other diversions, some merely to enjoy that half hour or so of school gossip they all found so enjoyable.

Billie found that a few of her friends still lingered in the grounds. Laura and Vi with Connie Danvers and Ray Carew were discussing the tennis tournament which was to be an exciting feature of the fall term.

These girls turned interested and speculative eyes toward Billie and her companion.

Edina would have avoided Billie's friends. She murmured something under her breath about having to get back to her dormitory; but Billie seized her hand and drew her on toward the group of amused and interested girls.

"You promised you'd do as I say," she reminded her companion. "And the first thing you've got to learn is never to run away from any situation. You've got to square your chin and look it straight in the eye."

Billie marched straight up to her friends, Edina's big, rough hand clenched tightly in her own.

"Girls," she said, in her forthright fashion, "Edina Tooker and I have decided to be friends. We are going to be the best of pals from now on. And I am depending upon all my friends to be nice to her."

There was a brief, uncomfortable silence. The girls did not like Edina Tooker. Nevertheless, they knew that if Billie took her up, sooner or later they would all be forced to accept her. Not too graciously, they bowed to the inevitable.

"Anything you say goes with me, Billie," Laura observed.

"Me, too," said Vi.

"Welcome to the fold, Edina," drawled Ray Carew.

"We welcome you as one of ourselves," added Connie, the sarcasm behind her words not too well disguised.

"I knew you would," said Billie sweetly, wanting, privately, to slap them all. To her new protégé she said: "It's only Tuesday, Edina. We will have to wait until Saturday, I guess, to get a day off and carry out our plans. Remember, we are going to make them all sit up and take notice. Until then, don't forget our bargain."

"I won't," returned Edina. She released her hand from Billie's and without so much as a good-by to the other girls made her way through the beautiful grounds toward the first-year dormitories. In that beautiful setting, she looked grotesque enough, as much out of place as the proverbial bull in the china shop.

"Well, I see you've gone and done it, Billie," sighed Vi. "I was afraid you would. But it's no use. You can't tame that girl."

"Like making friends with a lion cub," observed Laura. "You never can tell when it will turn and rend you with its fangs. That sounds a bit far-fetched, but I guess you catch my meaning."

Billie shook her head.

"You're dead wrong, all of you. Edina isn't a bit like that. She is headstrong and untamed, I'll admit; but at heart she's very much like the rest of us, wanting what we want and desperately anxious for an education."

Ray Carew's mocking laugh floated on the darkness.

"I hadn't an idea you were so credulous, Billie. The girl is nothing but a savage. If you try to help that sort of person you will only get your trouble for your pains. I'm warning you."

It was being slowly borne in upon Billie Bradley that she was alone in her championship of the strange, lonely girl from Oklahoma. Her friends, the girls upon whom she depended for understanding and support in what she had come to regard as an interesting and even exciting experiment, were subtly, but none the less decidedly, ranging themselves against her.

She turned to Connie Danvers.

"Do you feel that way about it, too, Connie?" she asked.

"I'm willing to be nice to anybody, if you say so, Billie. But I can't help thinking you are making a mistake, taking up this freak girl from Oklahoma. It seems to me you are letting yourself in for a heap of trouble."

"You feel that way about it, too, Vi?"

"'Fraid I do, Billie. Though I'll try to be nice to her, if you say so."

"And you, Laura?"

"You will never be able to make anything of that sort of girl, Billie. She has nothing in common with the rest of us. If you try to take her up, you will be only wasting your time. I feel sure of it."

Billie was silent for a moment. She was troubled and hurt, but the defection of her friends in no wise altered her determination to help the strange, wild, half-tamed girl from Oklahoma.

"Very well," she said quietly. "I am glad to know how you all stand, anyway. From now on, it will be my business to prove you wrong!"

As Billie limped up the gravel path alone, there was a curious weight upon her spirit. The disapproval of her friends was a new experience to her. Even Vi and Laura had deserted.

"I'll show them I can make something of Edina Tooker!" she told herself. "I'll make them admit it! I've got to now, to justify myself."

CHAPTER IX
THE EXPERIMENT

BILLIE BRADLEY awoke next morning with the same curious weight upon her spirit. Her mental depression was augmented by bodily discomfort that had grown no less overnight.

Every muscle in her body was strained and there were big, black bruises on her arms and legs, some of them as big as the palm of her hand.

"You *will* go picking goldenrod!" gibed Laura with sympathetic interest, watching Billie's painful effort to dress herself. "Next time you feel in the humor to visit Goldenrod Point———"

"I'll run the other way," said Billie, with a grimace. "Bother! I wanted to get out on the courts for practice to-day."

"From the look of those arms and legs, it will be many a day before you can swing a wicked racket, Billie," observed Vi. "Here, I'll help you with that stocking. Give me a chance to show what an excellent lady's maid I'd make."

Between them, they managed to get Billie dressed in time for breakfast. It was not until the bell rang and there was a general exodus into the corridors from the dormitory that Laura broached the subject that was uppermost in the minds of them all.

"How about this lion cub from Arizona———"

"Oklahoma," Billie corrected, a trifle frigidly.

"Well, Oklahoma, then. You aren't really going to wish her on the crowd, are you, Billie? If you insist, the girls will take her up for your sake, but there will be trouble. I feel it in my bones."

"I have no intention of wishing her on anyone," retorted Billie coldly. "The girl saved my life and I am going to help her to be happy here at Three Towers Hall, if such a thing is possible. You girls may do as you like."

Vi put an arm about Billie's shoulders.

"Don't be sore, Billie. If I can't share your enthusiasm for this wild girl from the West, I am quite willing to admit that you are probably right and I'm wrong. Anyway, perhaps it's worth giving it a whirl."

With such tepid support, Billie was forced to be content.

On the way to the breakfast hall they passed Amanda Peabody and Eliza Dilks. The latter called to Billie and reminded her jeeringly not to forget that she had a date with Debsy at ten o'clock that morning.

Billie flushed and pressed her lips tight together to prevent a sharp retort.

"Some people never get enough," she said in a low voice to Laura and Vi as they entered the dining hall. "So far we have beaten Amanda and her Shadow at every game they have ever tried to play with us, and still they come around looking for more trouble."

Across the length of the hall, Billie's eyes sought and found Edina Tooker. A look flashed between the two girls that was observed by more than one curious pair of eyes in that room.

Billie's look seemed to say:

"Hold on! Have courage. I am going to fulfill my promise."

While Edina, still a figure of fun in her outrageous clothes, seemed to respond:

"I'm depending on you. Don't fail me. You're my only hope."

That was the beginning of a period of acute discomfort for Billie Bradley.

It began with Miss Debbs' decision to give Billie two demerits, instead of one. Billie could never quite understand the reason, except that Miss Debbs was thorough in everything she undertook, including her methods of discipline.

Billie knew that the punishment was too severe, totally out of proportion to her fault. For a time she even considered taking her grievance to Miss Walters, the white-haired, gracious head of Three Towers Hall, adored by the girls and universally respected for her fine sense of justice.

Billie finally decided against this, however, accepting the unjust punishment with mental reservations and the determination to earn no more demerits during the remainder of the fall term.

To add to Billie's discomfort, Edina took to following her about like a humble and adoring shadow. Unpleasant Edina could be, and often was—snappish and curt, even downright rude—but never so to Billie. Her outspoken devotion was embarrassing; yet, in her secret heart, Billie could not but be gratified by it.

Edina was known among the girls as "Billie's little lamb," or "Billie's lion cub."

If Billie was sensitive to the only partially disguised amusement that followed them wherever they went, Edina was even more so.

She noticed, even before Billie did, that subtle drawing off of the other girls, even from their adored Billie. Edina spoke of this one day, in her clumsy, blundering way.

"You're gettin' yourself in a heap of trouble, tryin' to be nice to me. I seem to make trouble for every one I—like. I'd best go back to Oklahoma to Paw and Maw and leave you in peace."

"Nonsense!" said Billie, eying her protégé sharply. "You aren't getting cold feet at this late date, are you?"

Edina shook her head.

"No, I'm willin' to stick. The girls ain't been so mean since you've been nice to me. I'm gettin' some book learnin', too," the round face shone suddenly with eagerness. "I don't do so bad in my classes."

"You are doing splendidly," Billie encouraged her. "I was speaking to Miss Arbuckle about you yesterday, and she said that if all her students were as eager to learn as you, her task would be much easier. She was as pleased as punch with you, Edina."

The girl's face beamed with a sudden radiant happiness.

"That sort of makes up for all the rest," she said eagerly.

Edina in this mood was very attractive to Billie. She eyed her with sympathetic interest for a moment, then said curiously:

"You've something on your mind, Edina. Out with it!"

"I was thinkin' about you," returned the girl hesitantly, stammering and flushing as she spoke. "The girls you go around with don't like me. Oh, it don't take a microscope to see that," with sudden bitterness, as Billie made a negative gesture. "And because you're nice to me they—they are sort of drawing off from you, too."

Billie was startled. In a vague way she had noticed some such thing herself. Was her friendship for Edina Tooker imperiling her popularity?

When she did not speak, Edina continued:

"You've been the most popular girl up here. It didn't take a microscope for me to see that neither—either. There's no use your sp'ilin'—spoiling—all that for me. I'd best go back to Oklahoma, like I said."

Billie roused herself. She laughed and her mouth compressed itself into a rather fierce straight line. This was Billie Bradley's "fighting face."

"I think you are wrong, Edina. I'm pretty sure you're wrong. But if there's a chance in the world that you're right—then I want to know it. Don't you see? I'd simply have to be sure!"

Edina was watching her with a half-fearful eagerness.

"Then you mean——"

"I mean we will go ahead with our plans just as we planned them!" said Billie. She jumped to her feet with swift decision. "I have already spoken to Miss Walters about a shopping tour to Fleetsburg." Fleetsburg was the next town to Molata, a fairly cosmopolitan place with several large stores and a theater. "Some of the girls want to go to a matinée and Miss Arbuckle is to chaperone them. We are to go in the school bus and may have the whole day to spend as we like. We will buy clothes and other pretties till we're weary. You and I, Edina Tooker, are going to have a very large time!"

Edina caught her breath. The wistful longing in her round, red face was pitiful to Billie. She caught Billie's hand and squeezed it hard.

"You're awful good to me. Seems like I never thought anybody could be so good."

"No thanks, please!" cried Billie gaily. "Anyway, my work will bring its own reward. When we return to Three Towers Hall to-morrow you are going to be everybody's ideal of what a perfect, modern schoolgirl should be!"

Edina's gratitude, her eager anticipation, warmed Billie's heart. She carried her mood of elation to bed with her and woke with it in the morning.

"To-day is going to be one of the most interesting I have ever lived through," she thought. "The look on the girls' faces when they see my new edition of Edina will be worth all the trouble. Only," her face clouded, "I wish Laura and Vi could share the fun with me."

CHAPTER X
A TRIP TO TOWN

FOR the first time during all the years of their mutual association and friendship, there was a rift between Billie Bradley and her chums. Edina Tooker was the cause of it, as Edina herself very well knew.

Laura and Vi did not like Edina. They saw her as raw, uncouth, ill-tempered. Edina, who was always one to return either friendship or enmity with interest, did not go out of her way to alter their opinion of her. She disliked Laura and Vi openly, and this they took as a personal affront.

The fact that their adored Billie, despite all that had been said and done to discourage her, still clung to her original intention in regard to this girl, they also took as a personal affront.

"It seems that she might consider our feelings in the matter!" Laura had exclaimed on one occasion when she felt that her patience had been taxed to the limit. "Can't she see that our fun is being spoiled by having that Edina Tooker dragged into everything we do? Why, Billie had her out on the tennis courts yesterday, coaching her, actually coaching her!"

Vi nodded and giggled reminiscently.

"I was watching," she confessed. "Edina has a service that would smash everything in sight if she ever should get it going properly."

"Yes, and she's death on tennis balls. She wrecked two yesterday and lost a third. It was a scream. Connie and Rose Belser and Nellie Bane were on the sidelines, laughing themselves sick. And all this time," she added resentfully, "I was dying to have a set with Billie myself."

"Not much fun for us," agreed Vi, with a thoughtful shake of the head. "You know Billie promised to help me with my math—I *am* worried about that, Laura, and with good reason—but these days she has no time for anything but Edina. Old friends don't count."

"I heard her offer to help you yesterday afternoon," Laura remarked.

"Yes, while that horror was with her," flared Vi. "Do you think I could concentrate on three unknown quantities with Edina Tooker looking over my shoulder?"

It was Laura's turn to chuckle.

"I could imagine easier things," she admitted.

There was a moment of silence, while Billie's two closest chums reviewed their grievances. Laura asked suddenly:

"What about this mysterious trip to Fleetsburg to-morrow? Billie's taking Edina, isn't she?"

"So I understand."

"Do you know what's on the carpet?"

"Haven't the slightest idea. Two or three times I've hinted to Billie, hoping she might have a change of heart and confide in me, but she's been as mum as a clam."

"There you are! Having secrets with this western coyote that she can't or won't confide to her dearest friends. If that's loyalty, then I don't know it!"

Laura took an excited turn or two about the room, then came to stand before Vi, her hands in the pockets of her sport coat, her chin thrust forward aggressively.

"I tell you, Vi, if it was anybody but Billie I wouldn't stand for it for a minute! I'm just about fed up with this lion cub! I wish she'd go back to her mountain cave where she belongs!"

This was Laura's angle of it, and Vi's. Billie's was quite different.

Angered by the open hostility of her friends toward Edina, hurt by what she considered a misunderstanding of her own motives in regard to the girl, Billie had repressed a natural desire to confide in Laura and Vi concerning her plans for Edina. While they felt that Billie had failed them, Billie was equally sure that they had failed her. So began the gradual rift in their long and loyal friendship.

Several times during the process of dressing on the morning of the shopping expedition in Fleetsburg, it was on the tip of Billie's tongue to confide, belatedly, in Laura and Vi. But the two girls, nursing their resentment, were cool and distant, assuming an attitude discouraging to confidences.

"Very well!" thought Billie. "If that's the way you feel about it, I'll tell you nothing!"

She went down to breakfast with her nose in the air and a hurt in her heart. She had counted upon Laura and Vi, and they were failing her.

At nine o'clock the school bus drew up to the door, and those of the girls who were lucky enough to have secured permission for a day's holiday in Fleetsburg came thronging out, all clad in their prettiest, faces turned with bright eagerness toward this break in the school routine.

The girls were like a flock of butterflies in their gay clothes and smart trappings; all save Edina Tooker who, in her mannish tweed coat, heavy boots, and queer hat looked like something out of a curiosity shop.

The worst of it was that Edina realized to the full the gulf that separated her from these smart, happy, "just-right" girls. Every amused glance in her direction was a keen shaft of pain in her heart. She clung to Billie as though the girl were her one protection against intolerable suffering.

Billie, herself a little dream of "just-rightness" in a coat of some soft, greenish-gray material, gray slippers, sheer stockings, a small gray cloche with a green buckle snuggled over one ear, felt her heart burn with indignation at what she considered the callous cruelty of her fellow students.

"Never you mind," she whispered to Edina, whose face was grim and more than ordinarily plain. "We'll show them! Coming back will be different. Oh, very, very different!"

Under her breath, Edina said fiercely:

"They're horrid! I hate them! I'll always hate them!"

Billie sighed. At that moment she realized, more clearly than ever before, how difficult a problem she had undertaken. The self-appointed guardian of an Edina Tooker could expect no easy time of it!

As the bus started off, Billie looked among the crowd that had gathered on the school steps to see them off. Laura and Vi were not there. They had not even come out to see her off!

However, she caught sight of Amanda Peabody and Eliza Dilks, standing close together, giggling, and pointing toward Edina Tooker.

Billie turned away. Her color was heightened, her lips set.

"I won't let anyone spoil this day's fun for me! I won't!" she cried, and was angry past all bearing because there were tears of exasperation in her eyes.

However, the morning was fine; Billie was young and about to perform a fascinating experiment. The school bus had barely lumbered through the gates of Three Towers and started out along the lake road before Billie had forgotten her vexation in eager anticipation of what the next few hours might bring forth.

The girls were all in high spirits, bandying jokes back and forth and laughing at their own witticisms until it seemed a wonder the bus did not rock with their mirth.

Billie took her fair share of the merrymaking, answering quips in her inimitable way until Miss Arbuckle herself began to smile and the driver of the bus looked back over his shoulder from time to time with a wide-mouthed grin.

During all the fun, Edina sat grim and unsmiling. The merry sallies were never addressed to her. Had they been she would not have been able to retort in kind. She was as aloof as a snow-capped mountain. Perhaps only Billie Bradley guessed that under her aloof exterior Edina was as much a girl as any of them and that she suffered intensely because of her inability to join in their fun.

The bus passed through Molata at a merry pace and rattled on toward Fleetsburg.

Billie turned to Edina, her face radiant.

"We'll be there soon. And then such an orgy of shopping as we'll have! I hope," she hesitated and regarded the other girl laughingly, "I do hope you have brought plenty of money with you!"

Edina looked anxious.

"I've brought five hundred dollars. Will that be enough?"

Billie was staggered.

"Five hundred! Why, Edina, what did you think we were going to do—buy the town?"

"Well—how was I to know? Everything these girls wear looks as if it would run into a heap o' money."

"So it does. Nevertheless, five hundred dollars should give us a pretty good running start! Here we are, Edina! Come along!"

There was a riotous exodus from the bus, and in the general confusion Billie nearly lost sight of Edina. She found her finally on the edge of the crowd, clinging to her pocketbook and looking scared.

"Come along," said Billie. "I've already fixed things with Miss Arbuckle. We're to meet the girls at the Busy Bee at twelve o'clock sharp. Until then, our time's our own."

When they reached the center of town, Billie paused and looked about her thoughtfully. Then her eyes came back from their tour of investigation and rested musingly on her protégé.

"It must have been fate that made us stop before this barber shop," she dimpled. "Come inside, Edina. You are going to have your hair cut!"

Edina protested. She shied like a skittish pony at the barrier. But Billie had her way.

"Either you do as I say or you don't," cried Billie sternly. "Do you want to go back to Three Towers Hall *as you are*?"

"No!" said Edina.

Like a prisoner marching to execution, she entered the barber shop.

CHAPTER XI
EDINA GETS HER HAIR CUT

EDINA TOOKER'S hair, released from the hard knot into which she had bound it at the back of her head, proved to be luxuriant and soft to the touch. The barber, a dark-skinned, effusive little fellow, was charmed with the color and texture.

"It is a long day since I have seen such a head of hair. And now it must be cut off, shorn like the wool of a sheep. Eh, well, it is the fashion. These ladies," with a twinkling glance at Billie, "must be in the fashion or die, is it not?"

The barber took up a pair of gleaming shears. Edina's eyes met Billie's in an agonized look of appeal.

Billie smiled reassuringly, but remained adamant.

"She is the boyish type, don't you think?" she said, cajoling the barber. "It seems to me her hair would look nice short, quite short, and maybe tucked behind the ear on the left side."

"Leave it to me," returned the little dark man with a flourish of the shears. "I will make her ravissant. So she will not know herself. Now then! Attend!"

At the first rip of the shears through her heavy tresses, Edina shrank deep into her seat and shut her eyes tight. She did not open them again until the barber announced in a pleased tone that all was finished.

"Will you please to look at yourself in the mirror, Miss?"

Edina looked, batted her eyes and looked again.

"It ain't so bad," was her final pronouncement. "But it ain't me!"

Billie thought the haircut a triumph of art. It was cut short in the back, fitting Edina's admirably shaped head like a soft black cap. In the front it was longer, but not too long, falling back from the girl's broad forehead like the sweep of a raven's wing.

Billie reached forward and tucked a lock of ebony hair behind a shapely ear.

"You have nice ears and you should show them. Ears are an asset these days, if they are not positively deformed. Pay the man now, Edina, and let's go on about our business."

The barber bowed them out with Latin gallantry—they being the only customers in his shop at the time—and Billie led her protégé to one of Fleetsburg's best department stores.

There they entered into an orgy of buying.

Edina, bewildered, silent, left it to Billie to do all the work, merely signifying by a nod of the head when appealed to that everything was proceeding to her satisfaction.

"Something for yourself, Miss?" the saleswoman asked Billie, with a hopeful smile. "I have some sweet little new fall models that will exactly suit your type."

Billie smiled and shook her head.

"I'm not doing a scrap of buying for myself to-day. Everything must be for the young lady," indicating the tongue-tied Edina. "And we want everything, from undies to hats."

The saleswoman glanced dubiously at the dowdy figure of the girl from Oklahoma.

"Everything must be simple, but smart," Billie continued. "A complete ensemble first of all, if you please—dress, coat, hat. We will pick out the shoes and stockings later."

The saleswoman's deference returned. Here was a young person who knew what she wanted, even though her companion did look like some one's poverty-stricken cousin.

"This way, please!" said she.

The next moment Edina found herself in a tiny cubicle just large enough to admit her and Billie, a chair or two, a tiny table and the saleswoman.

The saleswoman, en route, had picked up two frocks and a coat of soft, rich-looking material.

"Take off your things, Edina," directed Billie, beginning to enjoy herself thoroughly. "This coat is adorable. I'd love it myself. What are you waiting for?" as Edina continued to regard her in a dazed way and made no motion to remove her dowdy cloak.

"You don't mean I've got to—to undress here—before a stranger?" stammered Edina and flushed crimson at the saleswoman's momentary and involuntary giggle.

Billie ached to echo the giggle but she only said gravely:

"Only to your slip, Edina. And we're all girls together. What difference can it make?"

As at the moment before they entered the barber shop, Billie had the impression that Edina was about to balk. She favored her protégé with a severe look and waggled a finger beneath Edina's decided nose.

"You do as I say, young lady, or back we go to Three Towers with only a haircut to show for our pains."

Edina hesitated, glanced appealingly at a ruthless Billie—and capitulated.

Off came the heavy coat. After considerable unhooking and unbuttoning, off came the heavy dress as well. Beneath the dress, Edina wore, not a slip, but a starched, old-fashioned petticoat!

Billie could not surpass an exclamation of dismay.

"Edina, you don't mean to say you wear *those* things!"

Instantly she regretted her tactless speech. Edina's crimsoned face grew redder. She bit her lip and turned away and Billie caught the gleam of tears in her eyes.

"Maw fixed 'em for me. She thought they was grand. I'm sorry if you think they are somethin' to—laugh at."

Instantly Billie's contrite arm was about the girl's shoulders.

"Dear Edina, I wasn't laughing, truly, and I'm dreadfully sorry for being so rude. It's only that a slinky, soft silk slip sets off your dresses so much better than a petticoat. Dresses are slinky these days too, you know. Still, if you prefer the petticoat——"

"I don't!" Edina had fought a battle with herself and was willing to acknowledge defeat. "Maw would want me to have what was right. She wasn't sure herself about the petticoats. You go ahead and tell me what to get. I'll do as you say about everything."

"Good girl! Then the first thing for you to do is take off that petticoat."

After a short, inward struggle, Edina obeyed and stood before the amused saleswoman and an interested Billie in a chemise and a pair of ruffled knickers. Billie was glad to see that, relieved of the greater part of her starched and bulky wearing apparel, Edina was slim. The saleswoman, too, was astonished.

"I brought you size eighteen and I guess you don't take any more than a sixteen," said she. "Well, we can try these on anyway, and see how you like the style."

Over Edina's dark, sleek head, the saleswoman slipped a one-piece sports frock, beige in color and elaborately simple in design.

It was too big for the girl, but one glance was sufficient to assure both Billie and the saleswoman that color and design were just right.

"I'll get her size in that," said the saleswoman to Billie, and disappeared.

Edina turned this way and that before the long mirror. She glanced appealingly at Billie.

"It looks grand—but it ain't me. Seems like I got to live with a stranger before I git used to myself."

"A mighty nice stranger, though. In that get-up, you're stunning, Edina—no other word to describe you."

Edina's pleasure in the praise was almost pathetic.

"You really think I look nice?"

"Stunning was the word I used," cried Billie gaily. "And wait till you see the rest of the things we are going to get for you, Edina Tooker. Why, you don't know the half of it!"

Before Edina could think of a reply to this cheerful prophecy, the saleslady returned. Over her arm were half a dozen frocks, size sixteen, two adorable coats and a shower of soft satin, lace-trimmed underwear.

Edina gave a little gasp and, like any other normal girl with a love for "pretties," seized a handful of the shimmering things and buried her face in them. When she looked up again, Billie knew that she had won her victory. The subtle magic, the touch of those lovely things, had accomplished more than all her arguments and pleading. From the moment, Edina was all girl, reveling in girlish things.

"I never knew just underclothes could be so purty," she murmured, reluctantly relinquishing the armful of loveliness. "I'd ruther have them than all the coats and dresses."

Billie laughed delightedly.

"I know how you feel. But, unfortunately, the dresses are a necessity. Now," with a little wriggle of sheer delight, "let's get on with the fitting."

The magic of those silken underthings had done their subtle work. Edina warmed to the spirit of the occasion. As Billie watched her try on dress after dress it seemed to her that Edina's very look softened; her nose became less dominant, her square chin less aggressive. In her eyes was a bemused, dreaming, feminine look that Billie had never seen in them before.

Billie thought of a phrase Amanda Peabody was fond of using. Edina had become "clothes-conscious."

After an hour of sheer enjoyment, Edina threw an appealing glance toward Billie.

"They're all so purty," she breathed, "I don't hardly know which to take."

Billie chuckled.

"That's easy! Why not take them all?"

The saleswoman threw Billie a startled glance, that at once gave place to eager hopefulness. Edina's glance was also startled—and hopeful.

"Dare I?" she breathed. "I never had so many clothes in all my life before!"

"That's why you need them now," said Billie cheerfully. "It gives a girl no end of confidence to have a complete wardrobe. And I'd add a party dress, or two, if I were you. We have school hops in the gym, you know, and once in a while the boys at Boxton give a dance. Yes, you will need at least two party frocks."

Edina had surrendered completely to Billie's guidance. She did not protest when the saleswoman—<u>voluble</u> now, and almost oppressively anxious to please—disappeared and a moment or two later reappeared with a mass of color and fluff over her arm.

Billie gave the frocks one glance and waved them aside.

"Something plainer," she said to the saleswoman, disregarding Edina's protests. "Something that depends entirely on color and line for its effect. We can't have Edina here swamped with fluffy ruffles and bead embroidery. It isn't her type."

"But I liked them," Edina protested, when the saleswoman had retreated uncomplainingly with her burden of fluff. "They were purty—almost as purty——"

"Pretty," corrected Billie.

"Pretty," Edina accepted the correction docilely, "as the undies."

"Pretty—but not for you," said Billie decidedly. "Trust me, Edina. I am going to make you a personage at Three Towers Hall."

Billie's enthusiasm was difficult to resist. Edina did not try to resist it. She permitted herself to be swept along by the new and entirely blissful experience of being able to buy all the lovely things she wanted at one time. The long-starved, demanding girlhood in Edina was finding expression.

The saleswoman returned with an entirely different collection of evening frocks which the critical Billie was good enough to approve.

"The coral one would look gorgeous on you Edina and the yellow taffeta. Try them."

Edina obeyed and was captivated. She insisted that she would take both the frocks of Billie's choice but remained adamant in her intention to try on nothing more.

"If I try 'em on, I'll buy them," she said, showing a grain of the good horse sense she had undoubtedly inherited from "Paw." "I've got more now than I could wear out in a lifetime of trying—unless I was twins."

Billie gave in with a sigh and a giggle.

"We've got to get hats and shoes and stockings, anyway," she mused. "Suppose we've got to stop somewhere."

The saleswoman, feeling that this was her lucky day, offered a bright suggestion.

"I can have hats sent up here to match the frocks———"

"One hat!" corrected Edina, putting down her foot. "I can't wear more'n one at a time, and that's all I want."

Billie conceded this point, having won so much.

"You might send up a few small shapes in beige or brown to match the coat," she said to the saleswoman. "Then I guess," with a hurried glance at her wrist watch, "that will be all!"

From the hats that found their way promptly from the millinery department to the tiny cubicle wherein Billie sat in judgment they selected one small, helmet-like chapeau that fitted Edina's head snugly and showed only one tantalizing lock of raven-black hair.

"Looks like I was scalped," was Edina's comment. "But if you say it's all right, that goes with me. Now," with a nervous glance about her at the extravagant numbers of her purchases, "what would you say I'd best wear back to Three Towers Hall?"

"The beige frock, the one you tried on first," said Billie, without the slightest hesitation. "Then that adorable brown coat with the fox collar and cuffs and the beige hat. Downstairs we'll get you shoes and hose and gloves to complete the outfit. Good gracious!" Billie glanced at her wrist watch again and jumped to her feet with a look of alarm. "It's past the time I promised to meet Miss Arbuckle and the girls. You stay here, Edina, and climb into that outfit. I'll be back in less than two shakes!"

CHAPTER XII
A PERFECT DAY

Billie Bradley found Miss Arbuckle and the girls impatiently awaiting her at the Busy Bee.

"We're starving!" they cried reproachfully. "What has been keeping you?"

"And where's the lion cub?" another wanted to know.

Billie smiled mysteriously.

"Just wait till you see her! You'd be surprised!"

Whereupon, Billie proceeded to "fix things" with Miss Arbuckle. This was not difficult, Miss Arbuckle being a friend of Billie's with consequent implicit belief in the girl's good sense and judgment.

"We haven't finished our shopping—not nearly," Billie explained, having drawn the teacher aside so that the curious and watchful girls could not hear what was said. "If you don't mind, Miss Arbuckle, I'd like to take Edina to lunch—just the two of us. After that we will shop some more and maybe take in a movie, if there's time."

"We—ell," the teacher hesitated, "if you will give me your word to be on hand to take the school bus back——"

"Oh, I will," promised Billie. "Thanks so much, Miss Arbuckle. It would simply spoil everything to—to spring Edina on them now."

A look of mutual understanding passed between teacher and pupil. Miss Arbuckle smiled.

"I suppose it would," she agreed. "Run along to your good work, Billie. I'm entirely in sympathy with it and I wish you luck."

"Miss Arbuckle, you're a perfect dear!" cried Billie gratefully.

She squeezed the teacher's hand, flashed one triumphant look at the group of curious, half-envious girls, and darted out into the street.

In the fitting room at the department store, Billie found a transformed Edina impatiently awaiting her. Billie paused in the doorway and stared at the wholly unfamiliar apparition.

"Turn yourself about, Edina," she breathed. "Slowly—that's right. My dear, you are a triumph! I'm proud of you—and me! Come along now and we'll get something to eat. I'm starving. Besides, I've got to show you off!"

Edina Tooker would never be beautiful. Nor could she even be spoken of as a pretty girl. But Billie realized as she looked at this new, tastefully dressed Edina that the girl possessed a native dignity and poise that was more compelling than mere prettiness. Her own prophecy was being fulfilled. The girl had become a personage.

Perhaps Edina read something of this in Billie's prolonged scrutiny.

"I'm just tryin' to live up to my clothes," she said, with a wistful smile. "They're the first things I ever owned in all my life that seemed to—to belong to me. I know I look different and, somehow, I begin to feel different."

"You will feel differenter and differenter as time goes on," Billie prophesied gaily. "You're a knockout, Edina. I can't wait for the girls to see you."

Into the eyes of Edina came a provocative gleam that was as new as her new clothes.

"Neither can I!" she confessed. "Mebbe they won't laugh at me now."

"They will be simply green with envy," prophesied Billie. "I am, myself. Just think of having all those perfectly gorgeous new frocks all at once!"

Edina chuckled.

"I can't get over the notion I should be twins," she chuckled.

The gratified saleswoman parted from them with regret and many urgent invitations to visit her again.

"If I did that often," chuckled Edina, "Paw would be bankrupt. As it is, I'll have to write him for more money. He'll like it, though," she added in that gentler tone she always used when speaking of her parents. "Paw always wanted to do things for Maw and me. He wants us to have the best, Paw does."

Laden with bundles, the two girls went below to the store tea room where they ordered creamed chicken on toast and apple tart.

Billie noticed that Edina ate carefully, picking up a knife or fork or spoon only when she was sure she had chosen the right one.

"Raw and crude enough," thought Billie. "But intelligent and eager to learn. Her new clothes will give her confidence. Meantime, I am having the time of my life!"

Their appetites satisfied, the girls returned with a will to their shopping.

Shoes were bought, several pairs of them, and stockings to match. Then Billie led her protégé to the toilet goods counter where they bought creams and unguents.

"Anybody'd think I was going to be one of them movie queens," Edina protested. "What do you suppose I'm going to do with that stuff?"

"Wear it on your face at night," Billie retorted imperturbably.

"Not all at once!" cried Edina horrified.

Billie glanced at her to make sure she meant it, then went off into gales of giggles that made passing shoppers gaze at her curiously.

"A little at a time, you silly! Edina, you'll be the death of me yet!"

"Well, I don't like the idea of it, nohow—anyhow," the girl persisted doggedly. "I ain't never—ever—had anything but good spring water on my face up to now and I'm not yearning to go greasing myself up like an Indian at this late date."

"You'll get used to it," prophesied Billie cheerfully. "You can get used to anything. Besides, now that you have all those beautiful dresses, you must grow a complexion to match."

"How you talk! A complexion ain't—isn't—like shoes and stockings—that it's got to match up with your clothes."

"It's even more important," said Billie firmly. "Don't argue. Come along!"

Laden with boxes and bundles, they found their way to a movie picture palace in the vicinity.

The scenario of the picture happened to be laid in the West—one of those blood-and-thunder films replete with villains, dashing ponies, lariats, and heroic cowboys. During the entire entertainment, Edina kept up a running fire of comment and criticism that provided Billie with more entertainment than the film, much to the annoyance of a dignified and portly old gentleman who had the seat in front of them.

At the end of the picture Billie glanced at her wrist watch and tugged at the sleeves of Edina's new coat.

"We have to go. If we miss the school bus we will get about sixteen demerits apiece and I'll be barred from boating and tennis for the rest of the fall term, and that I could never stand! We'll have to bolt for it."

Edina was seized by sudden panic.

"I don't want to go," she said, in a strained, tight voice. "I feel such a fool, all togged out like this! I—I'd ruther stay here in the dark!"

CHAPTER XIII
EDINA SCORES

FOR a moment, Billie Bradley lost patience with her protégé.

"Don't be silly!" she cried sharply. "Here I spend a whole day trying to make you presentable and you tell me you'd rather stay here in the dark. Do hurry, Edina. I tell you, we've only just time to make the bus."

Edina got up—and a dozen packages scattered over the floor! She stooped to pick them up and bumped her head into the head of the old gentleman in front who turned to glare at her wrathfully.

With an exclamation of annoyance, Billie helped gather up the scattered purchases of the afternoon and after an interminable delay the girls got to the street.

"We've got to run," gasped Billie. "If we miss that bus, it's all up with us. I promised Miss Arbuckle——" The sentence went unfinished, for at the next street corner they came in sight of the bus. Miss Arbuckle and the girls stood beside it, talking animatedly. Billie guessed from their gestures that she and Edina were the topic of conversation.

Billie had been almost running. Now she slowed her pace and glanced imperatively at Edina.

"Pull your hat down and put the collar of your coat up a little," she ordered. "That's right! You look swell! Act as if you knew it."

That was all very well for Billie Bradley, thought poor Edina; but Billie could scarcely be expected to know how it felt to be dressed up like a tailor's dummy and set in a window to be stared at!

Unconsciously Edina's face assumed the old, grim expression of defiance. She was the "lion cub" dressed up.

With her accustomed tact and kind-heartedness, Miss Arbuckle assumed charge of the situation. With the gesture of a motherly hen scattering her chicks, she shooed the staring, curious girls into the bus, so that when Billie and her companion reached it, there was no one on the sidewalk.

Billie was in fine spirits again.

"Follow me," she called to Edina. "And be sure to pick up the packages I drop! It will be a mercy if we get back to Three Towers with half the things we've bought."

As Billie and Edina entered the bus, all eyes were turned upon Billie's companion.

The moment of amazed silence that greeted the apparition of this new Edina Tooker was a genuine tribute to Billie's accomplishment.

"Hello, everybody!" Billie called gaily. "Edina and I have been shopping and we've bought the most marvelous things—dozens of pretty frocks and other things. Wait till you see!"

So Billie carried the battle into the enemy's territory. By this bold stroke she practically forced the girls to take sides either for or against her new friend and protégé. By it Billie said, though not in so many words:

"You must either accept Edina or reject her—and by rejecting her, you will reject me also."

If Billie had not possessed quite so strong a hold upon the affection and esteem of her schoolmates, it is quite possible that this bold bid in Edina's interest would have gone for nothing.

However, the girls loved Billie, and this new Edina Tooker in the marvelous clothes was certainly far more attractive than the old Edina. Then, too, there was the talk of new frocks—dozens of them, Billie had said.

The atmosphere became more friendly. One could almost feel it thaw.

Jessie Brewer, a diminutive blonde with round face and infantile blue eyes, turned the scale in Edina's favor.

"You look stunning," said Jessie, generously going all the way now that she had decided on surrender. "That coat is perfectly sweet. If I'm good, will you let me have a lend of it sometime?"

The request, with its tacit acknowledgment of equality, took Edina's breath away.

"Sure," she stammered. "Any—any time you like!"

Amazingly, miraculously, Edina found herself the center of interest for the first time since her advent at Three Towers Hall—for the first time in all her hard, drab young life.

The ice once broken, the girls were eager to hear about her purchases. At first Edina was unwilling to talk and Billie answered for her; but gradually the girl's reticence broke beneath the friendly battery of questions. She found herself answering in a perfectly natural way—not only that, but embellishing the events of the day with a dry humor that captivated her audience.

Some of her packages were opened by the more curious among the girls and passed from hand to hand for comment and inspection.

"Better watch these girls, Edina," laughed Billie. "They are apt to descend upon your purchases like a swarm of hungry locusts———"

"I may be hungry, but I'm no locust," said a dark-haired girl, who was sniffing curiously at a jar of cold cream with an exotic label and a delicious fragrance. "Anyway, I'm sure Edina won't mind if I just take a dab of this stuff."

"Take the whole thing, if you want it," Edina offered largely; but Billie gave a little squeal of protest.

"No use giving away everything you own, even if your father has struck oil on that property of his and is making money hand over fist. Take that jar of cream away, Edina, before Jessie eats it. She thinks it's for dessert."

So Billie skillfully implanted the notion that Edina was already very rich and growing richer fast. Among those who had snubbed the girl from the West, this would have a disciplinary effect, she thought, and those who were disposed to friendliness toward the new Edina would not be greatly affected by it, anyway.

She could see that the girls were impressed. Edina herself appeared somewhat startled by this frank statement of her fortunes.

"You shouldn't 'a' done that," she whispered to Billie in the flurry of getting packages together for the exodus at Three Towers Hall. "I ain't exactly superstitious, but seems like I don't like to talk too much about Paw's money."

Billie was sincerely surprised.

"It was true, wasn't it, what you told me about his oil well?"

"True as rain. But Paw's luck's been so uncertain that I can't hardly believe he has really struck it rich at last. Seems like if I talk too much about it, all his good fortune might bust up into thin air like them—those—soap bubbles you make with a pipe. I'm just being superstitious," she added, with an apologetic grin. "You ain't got no—any—call to listen to me."

As the bus turned into the long graveled drive leading to Three Towers Hall and the girls began to scramble headlong from it, Edina caught Billie's hand gratefully in a rough paw.

"It's been the best day I ever spent," she muttered. "Thanks—a lot."

Billie smiled and returned the pressure of Edina's hand.

"I think we've broken the ice. From now on, it's up to you."

Billie went on across the school grounds in a thoughtful mood.

The day had been an unqualified success. She had done just exactly what she wanted to do. Yet she felt depressed, deserted and forlorn.

"I'm the world's prize idiot," she scolded herself. "I'm tired and I probably need my dinner."

However, in her heart, she knew exactly what was wrong with her. She was unhappy because neither Laura nor Vi had come out to greet the school bus.

Were they still angry with her? Was the friendship she had thought so strong and fine, that had been a source of happiness to her ever since her childhood, to break up in this manner?

"All over a stranger, too," she thought wearily. "Edina has scarcely any claim on my affections. I'm grateful to her for saving my life that awful day at the lake. I'm grateful to her and sorry for her, that's all. But Laura and Vi——" She let the thought trail off.

In the hall she pulled off her tight hat and was conscious of immediate relief. How her head did ache!

She went up quietly to her room, exchanging greetings with the girls she met on the way. She opened the door softly and stopped as though transfixed.

On her bed lay Vi Farrington, face downward. She was sobbing as though her heart would break!

CHAPTER XIV
AN OLD ENEMY

IN a moment, Billie Bradley forgot her own weariness and the fact that her head ached worse than ever. She ran to the bed and flung herself to her knees beside the sobbing girl.

"Vi! Vi Farrington! What is it, dear?"

Vi gave a sharp exclamation and sat up, trying to dry her eyes on her pocket handkerchief.

"Oh, it's you! I didn't mean any one to catch me at this baby trick, Billie, truly I never did. But I'm so wretched."

"What about?"

Vi eyed her fiercely and accepted the clean handkerchief that Billie thrust into her hands.

"You, for one thing. You have been perfectly horrid, Billie Bradley, with that wild girl of yours and never having even half an eye for the rest of us——"

"Vi, you silly! I never——"

"Yes, you have! Don't you suppose I know? And then it's that wretched math. I—I've gone and done it again."

Vi threatened to dissolve in tears and Billie shook her rudely.

"Done what again? Don't you dare cry——"

"Failed, of course. What did you suppose? Miss Walters called me into the office to-day and she said, oh, B-Billie—I—I can't tell you!"

"You've got to tell me," returned Billie. "Go on, dear. What did Miss Walters say?"

"Well, she told me if I didn't do better in my math she would have to write a note home to Dad. Can you imagine Dad getting a note like that, Billie—or Mother? It would just about k-kill them! And I'm so perfectly d-dumb at figures!"

Billie got up and began to walk about the room. She took off her coat and smoothed back her hair while Vi watched her with tear-dimmed eyes.

"B-Billie, aren't you going to do something?"

"Nothing else, but!" returned Billie cheerfully. "I'm merely clearing the decks for action. Suppose you get out your books and papers and things and we'll try to find out what's wrong. I reckon we'll get to the root of this matter in a jiffy."

"Oh, B-Billie! When you talk like that I know that everything is going to be all right. If you will only help——"

Billie glanced up briefly into Vi's tear-stained face.

"You knew I'd help, didn't you, Vi?"

Vi's glance wavered, fell.

"I know I've been a fool, Billie. But I did think you were sort of sidetracking Laura and me for that wild and woolly Edina Tooker."

Billie shook her head reproachfully.

"You didn't really think that, Vi. Not in your heart. Now, let's get down to business."

It was so that Laura found them, some time later, heads close together, working out a problem in algebra.

"Say, you two, don't you know it's almost time for the supper bell to ring?"

"Don't bother us!" muttered Vi. "We've almost got it. There! There, that's the right answer, isn't it, Billie? Did I get it?"

"You did!" Billie's smile was congratulatory. "And in record time, too. We're coming on, Vi!"

She glanced up to find Laura's eyes fixed upon her curiously.

"Billie Bradley, what have you done to Edina? I met her in the hall downstairs. She isn't the same person at all."

Billie smiled enigmatically.

"Clothes do make a difference!" she observed.

That was the beginning of the old status between the three chums. It was the beginning of many things, especially for Edina.

Billie's friendship, her new clothes, and the general belief that her father was rapidly becoming a fabulously rich man, all these things conspired to lift Edina from obscurity to an enviable position among her schoolmates. She was sincerely liked by some, tolerated by many, and toadied to by a few who thought that she might some day become a powerful and colorful influence in the school life of Three Towers Hall.

In other words, as Billie had predicted, Edina was rapidly becoming a personage.

To be sure, there were some who still disliked and distrusted the girl from Oklahoma, decrying her rough language and crude ways. Among this small minority were Rose Belser and Ray Carew, who stood, figuratively speaking, upon the fringe of the crowd, skeptically looking on at this transformation of Edina Tooker.

"No good will come of it, Billie," Rose said, more than once. "You may tame the lion cub; but underneath, it remains a lion cub just the same. Some day it will begin to scratch and claw. Then—look out!"

About this time an incident occurred that afforded Billie a good deal of amusement and Edina no little satisfaction.

The girls spent much of their recreation time on Lake Molata during the pleasant fall weather, boating and, weather permitting, swimming from the end of the dock.

Billie attempted to initiate Edina into these water sports, much to the not-too-well disguised amusement of her fellow students. Edina disliked the water. She could not swim and she was not keen about rowing—that is, she was not keen about it until she found that Billie was.

This is how it came about.

One day while Billie and Edina were rowing in desultory fashion some distance from the dock, they were overhauled by Ray Carew and Rose Belser in a boat, the twin of theirs.

"Give you a race," called Rose, as she had called many times before when Laura or Vi had been in the boat with Billie. However, Edina was neither Laura nor Vi, a fact of which Rose Belser was well and mischievously aware. Edina rowed with a stroke all her own and possessed a positive genius for entangling her oar with that of her stroke mate.

Still Billie could not refuse the challenge.

"All right, race you to the island!" she returned.

"But, Billie!" cried Edina, aghast, "you oughtn't to've said that. I can't row!"

"Stop talking!" Billie commanded, her jaw set. "Stop talking and row!"

Such rowing! Edina's oar did everything but stroke the water. It sat upon the top of it, it splashed spray into the boat, it entangled itself with Billie's. By the time Ray and Rose had reached the island, Billie's boat had succeeded in turning its nose about and was headed the other way!

That incident was a lesson to Billie. She told Edina firmly:

"You've got to learn to row. That's all there is to it. The sooner we begin the better."

"All right," returned Edina resignedly. "Anything you say."

This was the beginning of much secret practice for Edina in a secluded cove, screened by much bright-colored foliage from both Three Towers and Boxton Academy.

Came a day when Billie admitted satisfaction in her pupil.

"The next time Rose—or any one else—challenges us to a race, we'll give it to her."

Their chance came two days later when Rose and Ray Carew again drew up alongside them and Ray asked laughingly if they cared to have revenge for the other day.

"Like nothing better," said Billie coolly. "What shall the mark be?"

"The big rock that juts out from the Point—if you can get that far," proposed Ray.

"We'll try it," Billie said calmly.

As the boat moved off to get into position for the start, Ray was heard to murmur:

"Some folks are just plain gluttons for punishment!"

Billie and Edina exchanged smiling glances and Billie leaned over to whisper:

"Remember what I've told you. Take it easy at the start and save your breath. Ready?"

"Ready!" returned Edina.

Billie gave the word to go, and they were off, swinging easily over the glassy water. For some distance they maintained the same pace, bow to bow. Then, by degrees, Rose's boat drew ahead.

"Steady!" cautioned Billie, as Edina's hand tightened nervously on the oar. "Watch my stroke and time yours with it That's it! Easy now!"

The other craft was two boat-lengths ahead. Ray shouted a derisive challenge.

"Now!" said Billie. "Keep time with me, Edina. Faster—a little faster. Now then! Let's show the speed of that good right arm!"

The oars struck the water in perfect unison, poised, struck, poised again, swifter, swifter, increasing that rhythmic stroke.

"Now!" cried Billie. "Put your back into it, Edina!"

With a magnificent final burst of speed, the boat swept through the water, reaching the point well ahead of its rival.

Billie waved exultantly.

"Well," she jeered happily, "you wanted to give us revenge, didn't you? And we are nothing if not obliging!"

Rose and Ray were generous in defeat.

"Whatever you have done to Edina, it's plenty," Rose admitted. "We other oarsmen will have to speed up if we intend to stay in the same class with her!"

"At least," said Billie, with a mischievous glance at her pupil, "we don't go about in circles any more!"

Despite this signal victory on the lake, Billie was far from satisfied with herself. Rowing was one thing—tennis was quite another. On the courts her old-time skill appeared to have deserted her. She had lost a good deal of her old speed and power. She was slower, and her opponents found it easier to catch her napping.

Even Vi beat her one day, which worried the loyal Vi greatly.

"What's wrong, Billie? You are absolutely off your form. Aren't you well?"

"Quite," replied Billie, and added with a worried frown: "It's my knee, Vi. Don't tell anybody, but ever since that awful day when I fell over the cliff, my knee has been acting queerly. Gives out under me when I least expect it. To-day, on the courts, I almost fell. Perhaps you noticed."

"I'll say I did. It was so unlike you that I thought maybe you were putting it on—just to give me a chance to win, you know."

Billie's brief smile flashed out.

"I'm not quite that generous. Hello—what's this?"

Billie looked up to see that Amanda Peabody had planted herself straight in the patch.

Billie said coolly:

"Did you want to speak to me, Amanda?"

Amanda's smile was malicious.

"Not particularly. I just wanted to congratulate you on the fine showing you made against Vi on the courts. From your performance in that last set, I should say that every day, in every way, you are getting better and better."

"It wasn't Billie's fault," Vi blurted out indignantly. "There's something the matter with——"

"Vi!" cried Billie sharply. "I asked you to keep quiet about that."

Amanda's malicious grin widened until it seemed to stretch from ear to ear.

"You don't need to be so quiet about it. Everybody at Three Towers knows that there is something the matter with Billie Bradley's tennis. It isn't any secret if that's what you mean."

Vi started to speak again, but Billie squeezed her arm sharply and drew her past the outrageous girl.

"I challenge you," Amanda called after them, her voice shrill with triumph. "I challenge you right now to a set, Billie Bradley."

As Billie continued onward to the Hall without even a backward glance, Amanda's mocking laughter followed her.

"You're afraid, Billie Bradley. You're afraid!"

Once inside the door, Billie turned to Vi. Her hands were clenched so hard that the nails bit into the palms.

"Some day," she promised vengefully, "I'm going to give that girl such a beating on the courts that she'll cry for mercy. You mark my words, Vi Farrington!"

"She'll get something worse than a beating on the courts, if you leave it to me, the horrid, spiteful old thing!" declared Vi furiously.

CHAPTER XV
AN UNEXPECTED DUCKING

THE trouble with Billie Bradley's knee did not improve during the days that followed. Although, assisted by her chums and Edina Tooker, she rubbed it faithfully with arnica each night, she still showed far from her old form on the tennis courts.

She was forced to suffer the constant taunts of Amanda Peabody and Eliza Dilks. Instead of making reply, she closed her lips tight and said nothing.

"Why not tell them your knee is in bad shape?" cried Laura on one occasion when Amanda's caustic comments had aggravated her almost past bearing. "You let her stand there and say all sorts of things and never come back with a word in your own defense. I must say I'm disappointed in you, Billie."

Billie shook her head stubbornly.

"I'll not excuse my failures," she said.

"Well, then, let me excuse them—or Vi or Edina here. We'll undertake it with the greatest of pleasure."

Billie remained adamant.

"It would be just as bad to have you making excuses for me. No, sir, if I have to take a beating, I'll take it right!"

Although her chums understood Billie's attitude and, in their own way, sympathized with it, no attempt was made to underestimate the dire effect of Billie's temporary indisposition upon their hope of victory in the fall tennis tournament, now close at hand.

"It isn't only Billie who may be defeated. It's our whole crowd that'll go down in the crash—at least, our pride will crash," sighed Vi to Laura one day.

"I know. But there's no use arguing with Billie when she's in this mood," was the response.

On the courts, Billie and Amanda Peabody had long been rivals. Amanda was a spectacular player with speed and power, but apt to prove erratic, especially when the play went against her.

Billie was steady, careful, sure, coolest in an emergency.

It was pretty to watch the two on the courts; it was always interesting; it was even apt to prove dramatic.

To Billie, tennis was a well loved sport. On the courts all personal enmity was forgotten, all private grudges temporarily wiped out.

Not so, however, with Amanda. This girl, while having developed excellent tennis form, was a bad sport both on and off the courts. She, unlike Billie, carried her private grudges with her and was only at top form when winning.

This year, however, it began to look as though Amanda Peabody would win. With Billie so far from top form, there was no one at Three Towers capable of giving Amanda "a good run for her money."

Billie regarded her chums with troubled eyes.

"If only one of you could train in my place———"

"Don't look at me!" cried Vi, in alarm. "You know I am a perfect dub on the courts."

"You are getting better all the time."

"It would take me from now to eternity to get good enough to beat Amanda. Don't pick on me, Billie. You know very well I'm out."

Billie looked at Laura, who giggled and raised her hand as though to ward off a blow.

"I'm good—I admit it—on the courts, as elsewhere. But not nearly good enough. Take Edina here," she added, with a mischievous glance at the "lion cub." "She looks like your one best bet."

Edina grinned.

"Me! I can bust the insides out of a ball when I hit it, but my racket and the balls, they seem to be just born enemies. They never git close enough together to be friends."

Laura chuckled.

"I've watched you miss more balls this week, Edina Tooker, than I thought there were in the world!"

Billie sighed and rubbed her knee reflectively.

"Well, it seems to be up to me. And I'm a total loss. I guess Amanda will walk away with all the honors this season."

"It's more than I can bear!" Vi stood for a moment in deep thought. Then said eagerly: "You know, Billie, I've a hunch about that knee. You've been working it too hard. I'll bet if you had absolute rest for a week, never went near the courts, it would be a heap more profitable than all this violent exercise you've been putting yourself to."

"But I need the practice," Billie protested. "My form is terrible."

"Your form is just as good or bad as your knee. Get that into shape, and I'm willing to bet your form will take care of itself."

"Sounds like sense to me," Laura abetted her. "Why not try it, Billie? I tell you what! Ted has been at me for a long time to get up a picnic on the lake. To-morrow's Saturday. How about it, everybody? Any objections?"

"Not a one, that I can think of," returned Billie, with a smile. "This is excellent picnic weather and we want to make the most of it."

"Before the lake gets frozen over with ice," chuckled Laura. "All right. I'll tell Ted it's a go."

Edina shied like an unbroken colt at the mention of boys.

"We git along together like rattlesnakes and coyotes. I don't like them and they don't like me no—any—better. You'd better leave me out of this here picnic. I'll spoil it all for you."

"Nothing doing!" said Billie decidedly. "You no go, I no go either. The boys don't bite and I'm sure you don't, 'Dina." With a severity, belied by the twinkle in her eye, she added: "You've got to learn to get along with the boys, you know. It's an important part of your education."

A few minutes over the telephone were sufficient to arrange with the boys for the following day's fun. A few moments more in the kitchen provided for the hearty appetites of a healthy group of boys and girls. Clarice promised to put up a hamper of good things that would make "yo' eyes pop clean out o' yo' haids."

"Now all we have to do," said Laura contentedly, "is to go to bed and pray for a clear day to-morrow."

Surely, the following day might have been an answer to any one's prayer for fine weather. It was one of those lovely early fall days when the sun warms the blood and the tang of crisp air sets it dancing.

"Oh, I do love this time of the year!" Billie's face glowed above the woolly white sweater she was wearing for warmth's sake. "It makes me feel equal to meeting and beating Amanda Peabody, even with one knee out of joint!"

"The way you look to-day, you could meet and beat any one with both knees out of joint," declared Laura loyally.

It had been decided the day before that the boys would row across from Boxton and pick up the girls at the Three Towers' dock.

Their part of the bargain was so promptly kept that the girls had barely reached the boathouse when they descried the fleet of rowboats coming toward them across the lake.

"There come Teddy and Chet———"

"And Ferd Stowing. But who's the fourth?"

"Paul Martinson, probably," said Billie. "Chet said he might come along."

Billie cast a sidelong look at Edina, and was quite satisfied with what she saw.

The girl from Oklahoma wore a white sport coat—recently added to her steadily growing wardrobe. The sport coat topped a white, fuzzy skirt and a silk jumper adorned with a flaming, scarlet tie. On Edina's feet were white sport shoes of an approved style. Her legs were encased in immaculate, unwrinkled white silk stockings.

The improvement in Edina was more than "clothes deep," however, a fact of which Billie was very well aware. The girl had acquired a new poise, a dignity which was very attractive. Moreover, her disposition had improved signally. She was not nearly so ready to claw and scratch as she had been a short time since. The "lion cub" was surely becoming civilized.

"You look stunning, Edina," Billie said. "The boys will love you."

Edina turned on her a look of panic.

"I'm plumb scared to death," she confessed. "I'd like to go hide in a hole!"

The boats scraped against the dock and with whoops as of Comanche Indians, the boys leaped to the dock to capture the girls and the lunch baskets.

Chet Bradley came first. He was burned a deep brown by the sun and was as full of animal spirits as a gamboling puppy. He dashed up to the girls, gave Vi a paternal pat on the shoulder, pulled Laura's ear and Billie's hair and—stopped short at his first sight of Edina Tooker.

"Hello!" he stammered. "I don't think I have had the pleasure———"

"Oh, Chet, this is Edina. She's very much the rage with us, and you'll like her, too. I'm counting on you boys to give her a good time."

"Righto!" replied Chet, grinning cordially. "We're fast friends already, aren't we, Edina? Come along, fellows," beckoning to the other sun-tanned lads. "Step up and be presented. If you like it as well as I do, we'll all have a very swell time!"

Edina was blushing furiously. Billie wished she were not, because it was unbecoming to her. However, the other boys seemed to like her and they were soon chatting and laughing together in a chummy and highly satisfactory manner.

The lunch baskets and the assortment of bright-colored cushions contributed by the girls to lend comfort to the trip were quickly put in place, and the girls invited to follow.

As Edina hesitated, lagging behind the others, Paul Martinson linked his arm through hers and led her toward his boat.

"You come with me," said the young cadet, with a masterful air.

Behind Paul's back, Billie winked mischievously at Edina.

"Without even fishing, you've made a good catch," she whispered mischievously. "Hang on to it!"

Whether this pleasantry confused Edina, or whether the girl, hating and fearing the water, slipped as she was about to enter the boat, no one ever knew. At any rate, she lost her footing in some way, pushed the rowboat outward as she fell, and plunged headlong into the deep water at the end of the pier!

"She can't swim a stroke!" cried Billie, and without an instant's hesitation followed the girl into the chilly water.

Billie dived for Edina but could not locate her.

"She has been caught under the dock!" Billie came up for a breath of air and dived again. This time she, too, came up under the dock. She bumped up against something that was only a fuzzy white blur in the water and cried in her heart: "Thank goodness!"

A long nail had caught in the wool stuff of Edina's skirt and held it fast.

Billie's lungs seemed to be bursting, but she worked at the cloth so frantically that the nail came out of the rotted wood.

As she felt herself begin to sink again, Edina twisted in the water and wrapped both arms about Billie's neck with the desperation of a drowning animal!

CHAPTER XVI
FIGHTING FOR LIFE

Locked in Edina Tooker's unbreakable embrace, Billie Bradley gave herself up for lost.

Edina was stronger than she, and now her strength was the desperate strength of mortal fear.

Billie writhed and twisted, striving to wrench herself free; but in her heart she knew her efforts were vain. Edina's grip was the grip of madness. She was dragging them both down to death.

Billie wondered why her lungs did not break with the fearful pressure on them. After a long moment of agony she almost wished they would break—to have done with the torment.

Suddenly something swam close to her. There was a sharp jolt and, through glazing eyes, Billie saw Edina's head snap backward. The hard grip about her neck relaxed, the weight that had been holding Billie to the bottom of the lake slumped away.

Billie felt suddenly as light as air. With all the strength that remained to her, she fought her way to the surface of the water.

Like a benediction, air swept into her tortured lungs. She lay upon her back and let herself float, gasping.

Edina was safe, she knew. It was Paul Martinson who had dealt the merciful blow on the point of Edina's chin, saving her life and Billie's. Paul would take care of Edina. Paul liked Edina——

Billie felt hands tugging at her, pulling her up on something that was hard and rough. The pier!

"Were you going to lie there forever and catch your death of cold?"

It was Vi's voice scolding, and Billie thought no voice had ever sounded so pleasant in her ears.

She was being pulled to her feet now, supported by loving arms, a ring of anxious faces about her. They were all scolding her, but she did not care. It was nice to have someone care whether she was alive or not.

"Edina?"

"Edina's all right. Paul has her. Now we are going to smuggle you both up to the hall and into dry clothes before you die of pneumonia, or something equally uncomfortable. Come along!"

While Paul Martinson ruefully wrung out his sodden clothes, refusing meanwhile to listen to a word of thanks, Billie and the half-dead Edina were hustled to the Hall for a change of raiment.

They approached the house by a circuitous route, carefully avoiding the groups of girls loitering in the school grounds. Entering by Clarice's immaculate kitchen and leaving a telltale stream of water across it, they hurried up the back stairs and by great good fortune managed to gain the dormitory unobserved.

"Now get out of those dripping clothes and be quick about it," ordered Laura, then added with a heartless giggle: "Two such drowned puppies I never did see."

"You needn't laugh," retorted Billie, stripping off her wet stockings. "For a second or two, there we were as near being truly drowned as I ever care to be. How about it, Edina?"

The girl turned a stricken face to Billie.

"It was all my fault!" she said, in a low voice. "You tried to save my life and I paid you back by doin' my best to drown us both! Seems I'll never get over bein' ashamed o' myself."

It was a full ten minutes before the combined efforts of the girls reassured Edina to the extent of persuading her to exchange her dripping outfit for a dry one.

"Tell me what you want to wear and I'll sneak down the back stairs and get it," offered Laura. "In your present low mood," she added, with a chuckle, "I'd be afraid to leave you alone. You might hang yourself to the nearest convenient chandelier."

"I might, at that," returned Edina, with a reluctant smile. "I don't know why you girls are so nice to me. I sure don't deserve it."

"People so seldom get their deserts in this life," chuckled Laura. She tossed an impish smile in the direction of Edina's long face and disappeared.

She reappeared a few minutes later with an armful of clothes and an exciting account of the adventures encountered in their acquisition.

"I just missed Miss Johnson and bumped head-first into Debsy. 'Must you dash about in this frantic manner?' inquired Debsy in a hurt voice. If I'd stepped on her toe she couldn't have sounded more injured! Here, Edina, these are all I could find. Hope they'll do."

"Guess they'll have to." Edina regarded Laura's offering without enthusiasm. "But I won't look near as nice as I did before. I spent an hour gettin' ready for that duckin' out on the pier."

The girls giggled hilariously.

"Love's labor lost," said Vi, wiping her eyes. "Edina, you are putting a lot of joy into my life!"

So they made a joke of what easily might have been a tragedy. When they rejoined the boys on the dock, Edina had lost much of her former self-consciousness and was ready to laugh with the rest over what she termed her "clodhopper clumsiness."

"Where's Paul?" asked Billie.

"Gone to change his clothes," replied Teddy. "He hasn't yet learned the art of falling into the lake without getting wet."

"Said he'd join us at the island," added Ferd Stowing.

They made a great to-do about launching Edina safely. Ted and Chet and Ferd held one of the rowboats close to the pier while Laura and Vi, doubled with laughter, assisted their new friend into the craft. Edina looked red and sheepish, but she joined in the good-natured merriment at her expense. Edina was learning!

"Stand back, Billie," cried Laura. "If this girl tries another high-diving act, it's our turn to dash to the rescue. Look out there! Ah, now she's all right! Come on, everybody. Let's go!"

The little fleet was launched safely at last—Vi and Laura both in Chet's boat, since Paul Martinson was missing.

They had gone only a few hundred yards from the dock when they saw Paul himself rowing toward them from the direction of Boxton Military Academy.

"Didn't take him long!" shouted Billie, from her comfortable place in Teddy's boat.

"Ain't boys wonderful!" Laura shouted back.

Having arrived at the island, which was well out in the lake and removed by a considerable expanse of water from both Boxton Academy and Three Towers Hall, the boys and girls disembarked and began the real business of the day.

"Take care of those lunch baskets," shrieked Billie, as the boat in which they were rocked perilously. "Ferd Stowing, you nearly dumped them in the lake!"

"Well, I can't take care of both the lunch and Edina," asserted Ferd, grinning. "Lend me a hand, someone!"

At the thoughtless words of the lad who would not willingly hurt a fly, Billie saw Edina color painfully.

"All this fun at Edina's expense has gone far enough," she thought indignantly. "It's got to stop! I could slap Ferd Stowing!"

"Why the frown, l'il Billie?"

Billie looked up to find Paul Martinson at her elbow, smiling quizzically down at her.

"You look mad enough to bite a nail in six pieces," continued the lad. "Just what appears to be wrong?"

An inspired thought chased the frown from Billie's face. She smiled at the tall, good-looking young cadet.

"Paul, will you do me a favor?"

"Dozens of 'em!"

"Then be nice to Edina Tooker, will you? Awfully nice?"

Paul looked quizzically in the direction of the girl to whom he must be nice—awfully nice. Then his glance returned to Billie.

"That shouldn't be hard," he said. "I think she's a ripping girl, really. Regular stunner."

"Oh, do you?" Billie's lovely face glowed with delight. "Oh, Paul, I'm so glad! That takes such a terrible weight off my mind!"

Paul's eyes rested questioningly on the pretty face for an instant, then he said in an odd tone:

"Billie Bradley, you are quite the nicest girl I have ever known!" With the words, he walked over to Edina and proceeded to monopolize her completely and thoroughly for the rest of that day.

Teddy Jordon came up to Billie as she stared after Paul Martinson's straight young back.

"What were you and Paul whispering about?" Teddy demanded jealously. "If he has anything to say to you, can't he say it out loud?"

Billie glanced at him fleetingly and laughed.

"Don't be a silly, Ted. Paul just promised me to be nice to Edina. And he has started right in to keep his promise, bless his heart! Come and help me get the lunch fixed."

The boys had brought frankfurters, a huge bag of rolls, butter, and a dozen ears of corn. Also they had brought the utensils to cook them in.

"Why did we bother with chicken sandwiches and cake?" Laura wanted to know. "If we should sit down and eat steadily for three solid days, there would still be some frankfurters left. Are you boys quite mad?"

"My good child, that remark just goes to show how greatly you misjudge our capacities," said Chet, busy over the fire. "I'm ready to bet right now that there won't be a sandwich or a frankfurter left—cracky, that fire's hot!"

"It's apt to be, especially when you put your hands in it," observed Vi unfeelingly. "Hi, Billie, what you got?"

"Letters," returned Billie, waving them. "I put them in my pocket before I left and promptly forgot all about them. Here, Edina, is one for you. Catch!"

Edina caught the letter just as it flew past her, in the nick of time to save it from landing in the midst of Chet's fire.

"Good catch," applauded Paul, standing close to her. "Open your letter, if you like. I'll excuse you. I'll even turn my back."

Since Paul kept his word, it so happened that Billie was the only one facing Edina when the girl opened her letter. So also it was Billie who rushed forward, alarmed at the girl's sudden waxy pallor.

"Why, Edina dear! what is it? Have you had bad news?"

Edina stretched out a hand as though to push Billie away. Her color returned in a hot wave. She spoke in a thick tone, wavering and unsteady.

"There ain't nothin'—anything—wrong. Please don't notice me. I'll—be all right—in a minute."

So it was Billie, staunch friend that she was, who turned the attention of the young folks into other channels, who kept up a running fire of nonsense, under cover of which Edina was once more able to resume command of herself.

The fact that the girl slipped the letter into her pocket without reading to the end of it did not pass unnoticed by Billie, nor the fact that Edina was distrait and silent for the rest of the long afternoon.

"That letter was a terrible shock to her," thought Billie. "I'd give almost anything I own to know what was in it."

CHAPTER XVII
THE MYSTERIOUS LETTER

IT was a lovely picnic. The girls could not remember when they had enjoyed anything so much.

The boys put themselves out to be entertaining, the weather was excellent. No one had ever tasted such nectar as those "hot dogs" cooked in the open, corn boiled in a big, blackened pot over the campfire and fairly dripping butter. Clarice's chicken mayonnaise sandwiches were not neglected, nor the cake with its filling of thick almond cream. Never was such a feast. The young folks ate to repletion, and then ate some more.

Only Edina Tooker seemed to have lost her appetite.

After the luncheon they sat around for an hour or two, too absolutely comfortable and lazy to move.

"Like anacondas, sunning themselves," observed Vi lazily.

Laura, half-asleep, opened one eye to stare at her reproachfully.

"How complimentary you are! I refuse to be compared to any snake—even an impressive one like the anaconda. Now, if anybody has anything more to say, please don't say it. I'm going to sleep!"

After a while they roused themselves sufficiently to make a tour of the island. Finding a little pool among the bushes, they made themselves crude fishing tackle of tree branches, a ball of cord conveniently produced by Chet from a roomy pocket, and a few fishhooks left by someone in one of the boats.

During an hour or two of fishing, Edina succeeded in hooking one poor little fish which was so tiny and, Vi declared, looked at her so pathetically she had not the heart to keep it. At any rate, she removed it with gentle fingers from the hook and flung it back into the cool depths of the little pool.

"A fine fisherman you'd make!" scoffed Ferd. "Here you hook the best catch of the afternoon and you aren't sport enough to recognize good fortune!"

Edina shook her head, answering his badinage seriously.

"It was too little to be any use, anyway. And I never could kill anything just for the fun of killing it."

Here was a new light on Edina's true character. How cruelly the girls at the Hall had misjudged her, thought Billie. At heart Edina was kindly and gentle, sympathetic and loyal. How gently she had removed the poor little tortured fish from the hook! And yet the girls still called her the "lion cub!"

"She's a darling," thought Billie warmly. "And I'm glad I've stood by her. I'd do it all over again if I had to!"

After a while the young folks resumed their stroll and wound up finally at the site of the campfire.

Here they discovered that their appetites had miraculously revived. Whereupon they fell upon what remained of the provisions and gobbled them up.

"What a swarm of locusts we are!" chuckled Laura, regarding the ruins of their feast. "I'm not sure that I'll ever be able to eat again."

"Until to-morrow morning," observed Billie drily.

The premature shadows of autumn were falling over the lake when they reluctantly decided that it was time to go back.

Like all good woodsmen, they cleaned up the scene of their picnic until everything was as neat and orderly as they had found it.

"I hate to go," said Vi, looking back longingly. "It's probably the last picnic we'll have this year."

"Probably," agreed Billie. "It's always a little sad, saying good-by to summer. And this year, what with the treasure hunt and Sun Dial Lodge, we have had such marvelous fun."

Later, as the little fleet moved slowly across the water in the direction of Three Towers Hall, the young folks sang, joining their voices in the sweet old melodies of Juanita, Suwanee River, and ending with the solemn and beautiful Now the Day Is Over.

When they landed on the dock the shadows had descended in a gentle mist over everything, touching familiar objects with a mysterious magic, wrapping the young folks about in a pleasant isolation.

In the shadows close to her, Billie heard some one sob. She turned about, surprised, to find it was Edina who had made that choking, desperate sound.

"Why, Edina! What is it, dear? Edina, tell Billie!"

"I love it all so!" said Edina, in a curious, harsh voice. "It's been such a wonderful day. I never knew what it was to be so happy!"

"But, Edina, that's nothing to cry about!"

"That—that's all you know! You shouldn't 'a' been so nice to me—you shouldn't, you shouldn't! If I have to go away from here now—it will—just clean—break my heart!"

Edina whirled quickly and vanished in the mist and the shadows, leaving Billie to wonder if she had not dreamed the curious interview.

"What's the matter with her?" Vi stood at Billie's elbow. "She's upset about something, isn't she? Could it be anything Paul Martinson said or did, do you suppose?"

Billie shook her head.

"Paul has been a lamb. I overheard him invite her to the hop at Boxton on the third."

"What then?"

"I don't know." Billie spoke wearily. Her knee was beginning to hurt again—and the tennis tournament was only a little over two weeks away! "Unless there was bad news in the letter I gave her to-day," she added. "I thought there was at the time. Now I am practically sure of it."

CHAPTER XVIII
THE GIFT CLUB

UPON the matter of the mysterious letter and its contents, Edina Tooker maintained a stubborn silence. Even Billie Bradley, with all her cajolery, could not win a single word of explanation.

"There wasn't nothing—anything—in it you'd be interested to hear," she persisted. "And there on the dock I acted pretty silly. I'd take it a great favor if you'd forget about it, Billie, and not ask me no—any—more questions."

What could Billie do after that but acquiesce? However, though the topic of the letter disappeared from her conversations with Edina, she was not at all satisfied with the girl's explanation, or rather, lack of explanation.

That the contents of the mysterious letter had come as a severe shock to Edina, Billie had not the slightest doubt. Proof of it had been in her face during that one unguarded moment beside the campfire; further proof, if any were needed, had been forthcoming during that other unguarded moment on the dock when the girl from the West had opened her heart to Billie.

That talk of leaving Three Towers Hall. What did it mean? Was there any actual possibility of Edina being forced to such a thing? Was something wrong with those oil wells out in Oklahoma? Edina had gone so far as to admit that the letter was from home. Had the visionary Paw of Edina's childhood overreached himself again?

Billie wondered, but, in the face of Edina's resolute silence, could find no answer.

Meanwhile, the girl from the West became increasingly silent and thoughtful. She rarely spoke unless first spoken to, and almost never smiled.

"She acts like a person with a dreadful secret," observed Vi upon one occasion when Edina had been more than usually uncommunicative.

"A worm is gnawing at the heart of the rosy apple," Laura agreed. "Maybe she is trying to keep the family skeleton in its closet. Most families have them."

Vi giggled.

"It's hard to think of skeletons in relation to Edina Tooker!" she said.

The two girls were in the study hall preparing their lessons for the next day. Vi struggled with her always-difficult "math" while Laura marshaled ideas for a composition on "The Relation of Science to World Progress."

Into this studious atmosphere Billie dashed like a breath of cool fresh air. With her were Rose Belser and Connie Danvers.

"Miss Gay is going to leave to be married," Billie announced without preamble. "A number of the girls are keen to form a gift club and raise some money for a really nice parting gift."

"You've got to be chairman of the club, Billie," said Connie. "Now, don't object. You are already elected—unanimously. Isn't she, Rose?"

"Of course. If you don't accept the chairmanship, Billie, there won't be any club."

Billie laughingly protested.

"Talk about being railroaded into a position——"

"Oh, hush up! You are already elected."

"There's the question of the treasurer," Connie went on. "Which, when you come to think of it, is even more important than the chairmanship."

"We will have to pick on someone with an honest countenance," chuckled Laura, adding, with a wicked air of innocence: "At first, casual glance, I can't think of a single person for the place."

In revenge, Vi tweaked her ear and Connie pulled her hair.

Rose observed drawlingly:

"Certainly no one would ever pick you for the place, dear child!"

"Stop squabbling and listen to me," cried Billie. "How would Edina do?"

There was a moment of dead silence while the other girls in the room stared at Billie as though they were not quite sure they had heard correctly.

Before any one could speak, Billie backed her proposition with argument.

"Don't you see, the girl is new here and she isn't quite sure of her position among us, yet. Giving her a post like that would be like a vote of confidence."

"I'll say it would," retorted Rose Belser drily. "It would go further than that. It would *be* a vote of confidence. Speaking for myself, I don't know as I'm quite ready for that yet, Billie."

"I'd stake my life that she is as honest and as worthy to be trusted as you or I," said Billie hotly. She paused and regarded the silent girls with sudden suspicion. "You don't mean to say you think she isn't to be trusted, do you?"

"Not so fast, Billie," Rose spoke soothingly. "Certainly this girl that you seem so keen about has never done anything to make us distrust her. It's only that she is new and it seems to me that an important post like this should go to one of the older girls—someone we know we can trust."

Billie wavered. There was justice in what Rose said. Still, the picture of Edina rose to haunt her, Edina pale and silent, Edina making a desperate effort to hide some secret unhappiness or fear. An offer of this sort now—it would be a vote of confidence—might be just the thing she needed to bolster up her self-confidence and help her forget whatever it was that was worrying her.

Very badly Billie coveted that post for Edina. What was the use, she thought rebelliously, of being one of the most influential girls at Three Towers Hall, if she could not have her way once in a while?

She turned pleadingly to the girls.

"If I am to be chairman of the committee, I want Edina to be treasurer. I have a very private and special reason for wanting it. Really, I have. Can't you girls do this much for me?"

When they did not reply at once, Billie shrugged and turned away.

"Very well!" she said coldly. "If that's the way you feel about it, I guess you will have to find another chairman!"

Connie groaned.

"Bring her back, somebody! Billie, you nit-wit, come back here! Rose—girls—if we have to take Edina to get Billie; we'll have to take Edina, that's all."

"You win, Billie," Rose surrendered. "I suppose if you proposed Amanda Peabody for the post, we'd give in just the same," she added ruefully.

"You won't regret it," said Billie earnestly. "I'd stake my life on Edina's honesty."

Later that afternoon a formal meeting was held in the gymnasium. All the students were invited, the purpose of the Gift Club explained to them, and their support solicited.

The business of selecting officers for the club was quickly disposed of.

Billie was accepted almost unanimously as chairman, Connie Danvers was elected to the secretaryship on almost as great a wave of popularity.

"Not that I want the place at all," Connie confided to Vi. "It's the most thankless of all jobs—and the driest. I don't know what I have ever done to have it wished on me!" Nevertheless, in her heart Connie was as pleased as any other normal girl would be at this proof of popularity.

When Edina's name was proposed for treasurer and promptly seconded there was a little murmur of surprise. Girls regarded their neighbors thoughtfully and began to whisper among themselves. Edina appeared the most surprised of them all. She was starting to her feet as though to protest when Billie tugged at her and whispered sharply:

"Sit down, you great goose! I want the post for you!"

Edina won from her opponent, the pretty doll-faced Jessie Brewer, by a small majority.

"Congratulations, treasurer," whispered Billie triumphantly. "I'm so glad, Edina. I knew they'd take you!"

When Billie rose to take the chair from Rose Belser, who had so far conducted the meeting, she was greeted by a prolonged handclapping and cries of, "Speech! Speech! We want a speech!"

When the noise died down a voice in the crowd was heard to say quite distinctly:

"It's all a fake! Edina Tooker was railroaded into the job because Billie Bradley wanted her. Well, they'll wait a long time before they get any of my money!"

CHAPTER XIX
A DREADFUL DISCOVERY

FOR a moment there was dead silence in the room. Then Edina Tooker jumped to her feet and faced the shocked, attentive girls. Her hands were clenched at her sides. Her face was fiery with anger.

"Who said that?" she demanded.

When there was no answer except a snicker somewhere in the crowd, she added furiously:

"You don't need to answer. I know your voice. I'd know it anywhere, Amanda Peabody! If you are trying to call me a crook, come on up before all these girls and do it! Come on! I dare you!"

When there was still no answer, Edina relaxed; over her face spread a look of contempt.

"You don't dare!" she said. "And I'll tell you why. You're a bully and a coward and the meanest girl in this here—in this school."

She paused for a moment while Amanda got up and marched to the door. Before passing through it, Amanda turned to fire one parting shot.

"You can call names, if you like. I don't care. They never hurt anyone. But I mean just what I said. I wouldn't trust you with a cent!"

When the door had slammed behind the unpleasant girl, Edina spoke to the group of students who had just raised her to a place of honor among them. Her speech was simple, direct, and to the point.

"If there's any more among you who feel like Amanda Peabody does about me, I'd be pleased to have you say so."

There was a dead silence that in many ways was more disconcerting than Amanda's accusation. It was Billie who came to the rescue of the new treasurer.

"You girls have elected Edina Tooker of your own free will. After what Amanda Peabody has said, I think it is only fair to give her a vote of confidence. Now altogether—three rousing cheers!"

The cheers were given with fair enthusiasm, thanks to the effect of Billie's personality upon her fellow students. However, Amanda's accusation had raised a doubt in the minds of many of them, a doubt that Edina was quick to feel and that Billie thought best to ignore.

The remainder of the business was quickly concluded. Miss Geraldine Gay, a pretty young teacher in the lower grades, was very popular among all the students of Three Towers Hall. The fact that she was about to be married to a handsome young man named Bryant Cummings lent an added glamour to the personality of the young teacher. The girls wished to give her a wedding present that would serve as a testimonial to Miss Gay of their affection for her and their good wishes for her future happiness.

"Now," said Billie when the selection of the officers had been concluded and the routine organization finished, "we will waive formality and pass the hat. Everybody ready?"

The girls were generous with contributions from their pocket money. When the contribution was counted the new officers of the Gift Club were amazed and delighted to find that the total amount was sixty-five dollars.

Ray Carew rose to make a suggestion.

"Madam Chairman, several of the girls have whispered to me that they won't be able to contribute until certain—er—packets arrive from home——"

There was a general giggle at this and Billie rapped for order.

"I think we quite understand the—er—financial embarrassment of some of our fellow members," she said, with a smile. "We have already decided to keep the fund open for several days. At the end of that time we will take a general vote as to what is to be done with the money."

Amid a clamor of voices the meeting broke up and the girls filed out, apparently well-satisfied with their part in the proceedings.

Billie, Connie, Laura, and Vi were left behind with Edina Tooker in the big emptied gymnasium. Billie thrust the sixty-five dollars in bills and change toward Edina.

"Here, treasurer, you will have to take care of this in the future."

Edina regarded the money doubtfully. Under considerable urging she scooped it up and deposited it in her new pocketbook.

"I never did like the job of lookin' out for other folks' cash," she protested. "Suppose I should lose it?"

"That's your job from now on," said Connie Danvers, with a shrewd but not unkindly glance. "I'd suggest you sleep with it under your pillow."

This advice was followed undeviatingly by Edina during the uneasy days that followed. Nightly, the new-made treasurer was haunted by dreams wherein bold robbers with masks and enormous forty-fives dashed out of dark alleys or around street corners, demanding her money or her life.

The fund grew astonishingly, and, with it, Edina's responsibility. On the fourth day after the election of officers it had reached the—to Edina—terrifying sum of two hundred and sixty dollars.

It was then that the new treasurer made up her mind to go in search of Billie.

She found the latter on the tennis courts, playing against Amanda Peabody. Edina frowned her disapproval. Billie had promised to rest that knee for the big contest, now only a few days off. This was the way she kept her promise, prancing all over the court with that hateful Amanda Peabody!

As though in answer to Edina's thoughts, someone beside her said:

"Isn't it awful! She just let that horrible girl pester her into playing. Now she will cripple herself, most likely, for the big match."

"How's the score?" demanded Edina.

"Even, two all, with this game thirty love in Billie's favor. It's been a lovely game to watch, but Billie is nearly all in. See how she limps!"

"It's an outrage!" cried Edina. "Why doesn't someone stop her?"

"Try to do it!" said the girl at her side, who had turned out to be Nellie Bane.

"All right," said Edina, her lips compressed. "I'll not only try. I'll *do* it! Watch me!"

As she started off toward the court, Nellie tried to hold her back; but Edina was not to be held. She paused on the edge of the court.

"Billie," bawled Edina in a tone not to be ignored. "Come here, please! I've got to see you right away!"

Startled, Billie faltered, fouled a perfectly good ball into the net and turned impatiently.

"Thirty-fifteen!" called Amanda.

"Billie, I've got to see you right away!" Edina's tone was urgent, imperative. It was as though her very life depended upon Billie's acquiescence. "You can finish the set some other time."

Billie shouldered her racket and waved to Amanda.

"I don't know what's wanted, but it seems to be important."

"I get the set then by default," called Amanda.

Billie nodded.

"Meet you again—soon," she promised.

Nellie Bane, who had been watching the by-play with great interest, heaved a sigh when she saw Billie and Edina leave the courts and walk off in the direction of the Hall.

"That girl, Edina Tooker, knows what she wants when she wants it," mused Nellie. "My, won't Billie be mad when she finds it's all a hoax!"

Billie was mad. She regarded Edina with such frigid curiosity that it is a miracle that girl did not turn into an icicle at once.

"You mean to say you dragged me off the courts when I was winning—when I was *winning*—just for a whim or because it amuses you to get me in bad with that horrid Amanda Peabody?"

"No, Billie," pleaded poor Edina. She was feeling the full weight of Billie's wrath for the first time and it made her miserable. "It wasn't for fun. I could see you were limping and I knew—well, I knew you shouldn't be playin' with Amanda Peabody just now and——"

"It seems to me I should be the best judge of that," said Billie frigidly.

"Maybe so. But there's good judges and bad judges and just then you wasn't bein' so all-fired good. I'm sorry if you're mad at me—and that will probably make you madder—but, like George Washington, I can't tell a lie!"

"You've put me in a false position," stormed Billie. "Amanda will say I was afraid to finish the set, and there won't be any one to disagree with her, since I won't tell her the truth."

"You can *show* her the truth next week," said Edina gently. "That is, if you rest that knee and get yourself into shape——"

"The knee is better," declared Billie. "It only hurt a little to-day."

"But it might have hurt a lot if you'd kept on going," Edina pointed out. After a minute she added: "Anyway I did have something important to speak to you about, Billie."

"What is it?" asked Billie listlessly.

"About the gift fund. It's grown so big it scares me. With that five dollars Jessica Holt put in yesterday it's touched the two hundred and sixty mark."

Billie opened her eyes wide.

"That much? I'd no idea!"

"I'm scared to death I'll lose it or something will happen to it," Edina went on hurriedly. "What I really wanted to ask you when I set out to look for you and found you on the courts was whether you wouldn't come into Molata with me. I could deposit the money in the bank there in the name of the Gift Club. After that," with a rueful grin, "mebbe I'd be able to sleep some nights!"

Billie glanced at the watch on her wrist.

"We have time now if we hurry. I think it's a good idea, Edina. Two hundred and sixty dollars! That's a lot of money!"

"We could buy Miss Gay a limousine with that," chuckled Edina, delighted to find that Billie was recovering her good humor.

The girls went in to get their wraps. Billie stopped in Miss Walters' office to explain where she and Edina were bound and to promise to be home well before dark, then went to the dormitory for Edina.

On the steps of the Hall they almost collided with Amanda Peabody and Eliza Dilks. Amanda swung her racket and regarded Billie with malicious triumph.

"You had a very important engagement, didn't you, Billie Bradley?" she taunted.

"Not nearly so important as the engagement I have with you next week," retorted Billie, coolly, referring to the tournament. "And that engagement I promise to keep!"

When they had passed beyond earshot of Amanda's mocking laughter, Billie glanced at Edina.

"You see?" she said. "You have put me in a very false position, Edina Tooker. While I have forgiven you, Amanda will take good care I don't forget!"

A rural trolley line ran from the suburban districts into the town of Molata. It being an ideal fall day Billie and Edina found the trip both pleasant and soothing. By the time they had reached the one bank the township boasted, Billie had completely recovered her good humor.

"Hand over your money and your troubles are at an end," she directed Edina. "No more dreams of highwaymen and thugs. Edina! Why do you look like that?"

The girl had opened her pocketbook and was staring stupidly at the contents.

"The money!" she gasped. "The money's gone!"

CHAPTER XX
THE ACCUSATION

"THE money's gone!" repeated Edina Tooker.

Billie Bradley would not believe it.

"You must be crazy, Edina—or you haven't half looked!"

She seized the hand bag from the girl's nerveless grasp and began to ransack it with eager fingers.

"It's no use," said Edina in a dazed voice. "I wrapped the money up in a paper and put it there last night. To-day it's gone!"

Aware that they were attracting the attention of others in the bank, Billie pulled Edina over to a seat against the wall.

"Here," she said. "We'll pull this thing inside out. We have to find the money, Edina."

The girl nodded dumbly. Tears overflowed from her eyes and ran down her face. Absent-mindedly she wiped them away with the corner of a new silk pocket handkerchief.

Billie dumped the contents of Edina's hand bag into her lap, scrambling them with eager fingers.

There was a vanity case—a newly acquired luxury, to the buying of which Edina had been egged on by Billie herself. There was a tiny blue-enameled pocket comb, a small purse containing a few pieces of silver, a shopping list, and a roll of bills amounting to ten dollars.

"That's all mine," said Edina dully. "The gift money is gone."

"If you say that once more, I'll scream," cried Billie. "Stop crying, Edina, do. You have got to pull yourself together if we are going to work this thing out. Let me think! You say you wrapped the money in a paper late yesterday afternoon?"

Edina nodded, twisting the silk handkerchief nervously between her fingers.

"You say that was the last time you saw it?"

Again Edina nodded.

"What did you do with it last night?"

"I put it in my trunk and locked it. It has a queer lock with a key that looks like a humped-backed old man. No ordinary key could open that lock!" She looked pleadingly at Billie.

"What did you do with the key?"

"Slept with it on a string around my neck. I sleep light, too. Nobody could possibly 'a' got that key off my neck without me knowin' it."

Billie nodded and was thoughtful for some time.

"How about to-day?"

"All day long my pocketbook has been in the locked trunk and the key was around my neck," said Edina doggedly. "No one could 'a' touched it without first knockin' me dead, Billie."

"Well, then—I don't see——" The amateur sleuth paused, temporarily at a loss. "It couldn't have been somebody in the street car, coming out, Edina? A pickpocket, you know. I've heard they are very quick with their hands."

"There ain't none of 'em quick enough to have got this pocketbook away from me," Edina retorted grimly. "Anyway, I was holdin' my hand over the top of it all the way—just for fear someone would get a hold of it."

Billie jumped to her feet. Her eyes were bright and her cheeks were almost feverishly flushed.

"Then if you are quite sure of this, the money must be up at Three Towers. You have dropped the money out of your pocketbook—perhaps when you picked it up."

Edina started to say that she could not possibly have done any such thing; but Billie was beyond listening to her.

"Come along," she cried, with feverish impatience. "We've got to get back right away—before any one finds that packet and makes off with it!"

Billie's impatience infected Edina. The two girls rushed for the street car, caught it by the barest margin, and sat twiddling their fingers in desperate suspense during the seemingly interminable ride back to Three Towers Hall.

Released by the trolley, they rushed to Edina's dormitory. As luck would have it, the long room was empty and they at once began a feverish search of everything in it, beginning with Edina's trunk and winding up by peering under mattresses and into pillow slips.

"Nothing!" panted Billie. She sat down on the edge of Edina's bed to rest "Edina! Edina! Where has that money gone?"

"I'd just about give ten years of my life to know," returned Edina.

She sat down on the bed beside Billie. Her hands felt cold but her head was throbbing feverishly.

"Billie," she said dully, "it's the end of everything for me here."

"Nonsense!" said Billie, and took one of the cold hands and held it tight.

"It is," said Edina. "They'll say I took that money, Billie. What's worse, they'll *think* I took it."

"I won't," said Billie.

"I know you won't. I think you're the only one here who really knows me. It's been a long hard fight with the rest. Now they will think I took the money and it will be the end of everything for me. I—I was beginning to be so happy here."

Before Billie could say a word of comfort or reassurance the door opened and several of the younger girls flocked in. Their talk and laughter died at sight of Billie and Edina.

"Well!" said a dark-haired, dark-eyed, pert little thing. "You two look as if you'd been talking secrets. What's up?"

Before Billie could stop her or could even be sure what she was going to do, Edina got to her feet and faced the curious girls.

Her eyes were red with crying, her fingers clasped and unclasped nervously, but her voice was steady as she said:

"I suppose you might as well know now as any time. That money the girls trusted me with, the money to buy the present for Miss Gay, I—I've lost it. Or it has been stolen!"

The news spread like wildfire.

Billie dragged Edina to her dormitory, hoping to protect the girl, only to find her own friends lying in wait for her.

There was a crowd already gathered there, a crowd that increased in numbers rapidly. At sight of it, Edina shrank within herself and would have fled cravenly had it not been for Billie's grip upon her hand.

"No use running away," Billie whispered fiercely. "It's far better to stay and face the music."

Ray Carew pushed her way to Billie's side. She eyed Edina coldly.

"I've heard so many rumors that I don't know what to believe and what not to," she said. "What is all this about the Gift Club money being lost, Billie?"

"I'm afraid it's true," said Billie gravely. "Only in my opinion it has been stolen—not lost."

Briefly but graphically, she gave an account of her and Edina's trip to the bank in Molata, of their surprise and consternation when Edina discovered the loss of the money.

Laura, who had taken a firm stand at Billie's side, turned to Edina.

"Didn't you look inside your pocketbook before you started downtown?" she asked.

Edina crimsoned.

"No," she admitted. "I was so sure the money was there I—I—didn't bother to look."

"A fine treasurer!" came shrilly from the fringe of the crowd.

"I should 'a' looked," confessed Edina miserably. "I'll never forgive myself for—for not lookin'."

Billie's grip tightened reassuringly upon her fingers.

"Hold fast," she whispered.

"Let's get this straight," said Ray Carew. "Your story is that you took your purse from your locked trunk about two o'clock this afternoon. You don't know that the money was there then, because you didn't bother to look," there was the faintest sarcasm in Ray's drawling tones.

"I'm sure the money was there then," Edina persisted doggedly. "Nobody could get into my trunk without breaking the lock—and the lock wasn't broken."

"Well, let's say that the money was in your purse when you took it from the trunk," Ray conceded. "You took the purse in your hand then. Was there anyone in the room with you?"

"No one except Billie," said Edina.

"Well, now, think hard. This may be quite important. Did you hold the pocketbook in your hand every moment from the time you took it from the trunk to the moment you opened it in the Molata bank?"

Edina pondered the question, brows knitted.

"I—I think so."

"Thinking won't do," said Ray inexorably. "Don't you know?"

Edina thought again and finally shook her head in miserable bewilderment.

"I can't be absolutely sure—I don't seem to remember very well. I'm practically sure I didn't lay down that there pocketbook for a minute, but——"

"Yes you did, Edina!" Billie cried triumphantly.

"Where—when——" stuttered Edina.

"You put it down on the table for a minute while you went to the bathroom at the last moment to wash your hands. Don't you remember?"

"I can't seem to think," replied Edina hesitatingly. "If I only could be sure——"

Ray Carew turned a serious face to Billie.

"Are you sure of that, Billie?"

Someone in the group snickered and a voice not hard to identify as Amanda Peabody's said meaningly:

"If Billie Bradley was in the room alone with that money, what was to prevent her making off with it herself?"

CHAPTER XXI
EVIDENCE PILES UP

FOR a moment there was such dead silence in the room that one could easily have heard a pin drop.

Then Billie said in a clear, hard voice:

"Are you suggesting that I stole the Gift Club money, Amanda Peabody?"

"Because if you are," cried Laura fiercely, "I'll settle with you now, you miserable sneak, once and for all!"

"Girls! Girls!" pleaded Ray Carew. "Don't let's fight among ourselves. What Amanda just said is too silly to notice. I think you had better apologize, Amanda. You won't be very popular until you do."

A murmur of assent rose from the girls, a murmur so fierce and insistent, that Amanda was temporarily cowed.

"Oh, all right," she muttered surlily. "Maybe I didn't mean that Billie Bradley did it. But the thing looks very queer to me, just the same."

The thing looked very queer to everybody. As the dreary days dragged by things looked queerer and queerer. The mystery grew blacker and blacker and the general interest and indignation aroused over the mysterious disappearance of that two hundred and sixty dollars amounted to a school revolution.

Many at first stood for Edina, partly for Billie's sake, partly because they could not bring themselves to believe that the girl from the West would deliberately misappropriate funds entrusted to her by her comrades.

However, little by little bits of evidence piled up against the treasurer of the Gift Club.

Nellie Bane came back to the Hall one day from a trip into town with information that blanched Billie's face and for a moment shook even her staunch belief in Edina.

"I barged into this shop to buy a pair of shoes," so went Nellie's breathless story, "and when the salesman reached into his till for change, he pulled out a five dollar gold piece." She paused and regarded the intent ring of faces for a long, impressive moment. "It was the very same gold piece that I handed over to Edina Tooker as my contribution to the Gift Club fund!"

A deep sigh burst from the group. Billie sat back and passed her hand over her forehead.

"But I don't see—That is, how did you know———"

"That it was *my* gold piece?" Nellie finished eagerly. "Well, here's how I knew! I said some idiotic things to the shoe clerk about how pretty gold money is—because, you see, I was suddenly anxious, very anxious, to know where that particular gold piece had come from.

"The clerk seemed willing enough to talk, and he said it had been paid to him just two days before by a stunning-looking girl who said she came from Three Towers Hall. You can imagine how I felt then!"

"Did you ask the clerk to describe this girl?" asked Billie faintly.

"Of course. And, girls, the description fitted Edina Tooker like a glove. It just couldn't have been any one else! Edina spent my five dollar gold piece for a pair of shoes!"

Billie got to her feet.

"I don't believe it, Nellie," she said quietly. "No matter how strong the evidence is against Edina Tooker, I never will—I never *can*—believe that she is a thief!"

She hesitated, started off, and then came back to them again.

"Let's put the thing reasonably. What possible motive would Edina Tooker have for stealing our poor little Gift Club fund? She doesn't need it. Her father is a rich man."

"So she says!"

Billie shrugged.

"It's the truth, just the same. You can look it up if you like!"

How little did Billie guess that in giving that permission or in making that suggestion she was lighting the fuse to a stick of dynamite!

One of the girls who had listened with interest to Nellie Bane's story went directly to her room and began to write a letter.

It was some days later that the same girl, bursting with news and importance, dashed into the midst of an "agitation meeting" that was being held in the school gymnasium.

Billie had been addressing the meeting, urging moderation in their treatment of Edina, trying to sound hopeful in her prophecy that the money would "turn up yet."

Into this atmosphere, already surcharged with conflicting emotions, dashed the girl who had written the letter on the memorable day of Nellie

Bane's story. Her name was Nancy Cutter and she carried another letter which she waved about her head as though it had been a flag and this the occasion of a celebration.

Billie's heart sank as she recognized, or thought she recognized, fresh trouble for Edina. She gave a hasty look around to make sure that the girl from Oklahoma was not present. With relief, she realized that Edina had decided not to brave the meeting. It was just as well. Billie herself had urged her to stay away.

"What is it, Nancy?" asked Billie quietly.

The excited girl shoved the letter into her hand.

"It's something about Edina Tooker. I thought you might like to read it, Billie!"

Billie shook her head.

"If it's anything against Edina, I don't want to read it, Nancy."

A chorus of voices rose in protest.

"Read it, Nancy!"

"Tell us what's in the letter!"

"Read it aloud!"

Happy to be in the limelight, Nancy faced the crowd, waving the letter over her head again as though it had been a flag.

"It's from my aunt and uncle in Oklahoma. I wrote them to find out what I could about Paw Tooker and his million dollar oil well."

There was a titter among the crowd. Billie clenched her hands.

"Meddler!" she cried, under her breath.

Nancy Cutter read slowly and distinctly from the letter.

> "'I was surprised by your inquiries in regard to Peter Tooker, my dear Nancy. Tooker is quite a character in these parts, a visionary, a dreamer, a seeker after the impossible. I was still more surprised to hear that he had a daughter at Three Towers Hall. It was the first mention I have ever heard of a daughter.'

"Now listen to this!" Nancy adjusted her attentive audience. "The best is still to come!

"'I believe there was some excitement for a while about a report of the discovery of oil on the old fellow's property. There was immense activity there for a time. But it is over now. Just yesterday I met a man who said Tooker's wells had gone dry.'

"There!" cried Nancy triumphantly. "I told you all that talk about Edina being rich was a fake."

Billie was on her feet, fighting desperately for her friend.

"I don't believe it. That letter is all a mis——"

She stopped suddenly, her eyes on someone who had just entered the gymnasium.

"No," a voice said, clearly and distinctly. "Everything that Nancy Cutter read is true!"

CHAPTER XXII
A RIOT

THE girls, chattering like a group of magpies and flinging curious, unfriendly glances toward Edina, had gone. Billie was alone with her in the big, silent, echoing gymnasium.

Edina sat on a bench, her hands clasped before her, a wooden, miserable figure.

Billie paced restlessly up and down, up and down——suddenly she paused in front of Edina.

"Why didn't you tell me, if you knew? You should have told me, Edina. It wasn't fair to leave me in the dark."

Edina nodded.

"I know that. I meant to tell you as soon as I heard from home that Paw's wells had gone dry. But, somehow, after tellin' such wonderful tales about him, seems like I couldn't bear to take them back. The truth," with a bitter grimace, "wasn't half so pretty!"

"When did you get the bad news from home?" Billie queried. She paused before Edina and regarded her intently, while proceeding to answer her own question. "It was the day we had the picnic over on the island, wasn't it? The day you read the letter I handed you and you turned so white I thought you were going to faint?"

Edina nodded miserably.

"Yes, I knew then that Paw's luck had gone back on him like it always had before. But I didn't say anything. I guess—I was holdin' on to the hope that it wasn't so; that mebbe if I waited and said nothin' for a few days I'd wake up and find that that news was only a bad dream."

Billie paused in her restless pacing. She appeared to have come to a decision.

"Everything appears to be just as bad for us as it possibly can be, Edina. But since you know and I know that you didn't steal that money there's just one thing to be done."

Edina asked without interest:

"What?"

Billie stiffened her back and a purposeful glint came into her eye.

"Find the real thief!"

Billie wasted no time putting her decision to work. She had never fancied herself particularly as a detective, yet now she set herself to the task with a will.

In regard to the stolen money, her thoughts returned again and again to that few minutes when Edina had abandoned her hand bag and its precious contents to wash her hands before going downtown to place the money in the bank.

Billie herself, busy with her own thoughts and still smarting over the fact that she had been tricked into leaving the tennis court without finishing that set with Amanda, had stood with her back to the room, looking from the window.

Billie was willing to admit that someone might have entered the room during that interval, opened Edina's bag, seized the precious roll of money, and disappeared without being seen by either her or Edina.

If this reasoning were taken from the realm of sheer surmise, if it had in it some elements of fact, then who could it be who had entered that room during the few moments when Billie's back was turned?

"That certainly is my problem," thought Billie. "A hard one to solve, I'll admit; harder than any I've ever helped Vi with! But I'll find the answer. I must!"

Of course, there was always the possibility that one of the students in the school might be the thief, but as Billie reviewed the list of her acquaintances, this possibility became increasingly far-fetched.

Amanda Peabody might have done it for spite, in the hope of discrediting both Edina and Billie. However, Billie knew the unpleasant girl too well to entertain any serious belief of her guilt. Amanda was a coward and while she delighted in small meannesses, would hesitate, Billie felt sure, before an act involving such serious consequences.

"Why, we could put her in jail for stealing two hundred and sixty dollars," thought Billie. She shuddered with dread at the realization that this same punishment might be meted out to Edina, provided the real thief were not caught!

"The real thief must be caught," she told herself, for perhaps the hundredth time, and went on with her cogitations.

The elimination of the students and the teachers narrowed the list of suspects to the servants at the Hall.

Clarice, the cook? Perhaps—though Billie was loath to suspect anyone who made such excellent chocolate cake. There were three maids and a scrubwoman who attended to the general cleaning of the dormitories and the study halls. Anyone of them might——

Billie swung her feet to the floor and stood up. For some time there had been the sound of voices beneath the window. The voices had steadily increased in volume until now they broke with rude force into her meditations.

"Sounds like a riot," thought Billie.

A voice, raised above the rest, cried shrilly:

"Arrest her! That's the thing to do! Maybe then she'll tell what she did with our money!"

Other voices joined in the cry.

"Arrest her! Arrest her! She's nothing but a thief!"

Billie lingered to hear no more, but, turning, fled from the dormitory. When she emerged into the grounds she found a large group of students gathered there. In the midst of them, badgered, desperate, stood Edina Tooker!

Billie set her lips grimly and thrust her way through the crowd.

The girls gave way reluctantly and pressed more closely about her as Billie took up her position beside the tormented girl.

"Get away, Billie!" one of them cried. "This isn't your business any more!"

Billie faced them furiously.

"I'll show you that it's my business!"

Her voice was drowned in a chorus of angry cries.

"We want Edina!"

"Billie can't stop us any more. Get out of the way, Billie!"

"We'll have her arrested! Then maybe she'll give us our money back!"

Billie was helpless. Although she flung an arm about Edina and tried by main force to push the girls away, they only surged the closer.

Hands reached out. They touched Edina, caught her! She was being dragged away!

Billie felt that she was in a nightmare where every sense was impotent. She spoke, but could not make her voice heard. She used her strength, and was powerless. They were dragging Edina away!

Suddenly a voice spoke sharply, authoritatively, from the school steps. Instantly the crowd about Billie and Edina gave back. The girls lapsed into sullen silence.

"I am amazed! I am shocked!" said Miss Sara Walters in cool, clipped tones. "Never before has it been my doubtful privilege to witness such a demonstration from these school steps. I trust that it will never be necessary for me to witness such a disgraceful exhibition again. Go to your dormitories and remain there until the supper bell rings!"

The crowd dispersed rapidly and faded away. Miss Walters disappeared within doors. Billie and Edina were left alone.

"You see!" said Edina drearily. "They are all against me, Billie. I don't believe there is a girl at Three Towers—except you—who doesn't think I'm a thief."

"It was dreadful—disgraceful!" Billie was trembling with reaction from her fury. "It seems impossible to believe girls could be so wicked, so cruel!"

Edina shook her head.

"They think I've lied to them. They think I've cheated them. They want their money, and you can't rightly blame them. I guess I'd best be gettin' back to Paw and Maw."

"No!" cried Billie. "You will stay here and fight it out!"

Many times in the days that followed Billie Bradley was to doubt the wisdom of this decision. Edina was acutely miserable; she was subject to constant snubs, slights, insults, at the hands of her fellow students. She became pitifully pale and thin and kept to her room whenever possible.

Billie herself was scarcely less miserable. Her fellow students made it quite clear that she was alone in her championship of Edina. The fact that she persisted in her stubborn course irritated them and made her something of a pariah, too.

Meanwhile Billie kept close watch upon the comings and goings of the servants at the Hall, hoping for some clue that would lead her to the real thief and thus exonerate Edina.

Billie found it necessary to replenish her wardrobe by a day's shopping in town. Having asked for and received the necessary permission from Miss Walters, she set off early on Saturday morning, determined to dispose of her shopping as soon as possible and return in time to help Vi with her always-difficult mathematics.

Having arrived in town, she went at once to a small drygoods store where she bought a dozen handkerchiefs and one or two inexpensive articles of underwear.

When she tendered the storekeeper a ten dollar bill he returned her a five dollar bill and some odd pieces of silver.

Billie was about to stuff the change into her pocketbook when something about the five dollar bill arrested her attention.

She looked at it more closely and a stifled exclamation escaped her.

"Anything wrong, Miss?" asked the storekeeper anxiously.

"No, no," Billie answered hastily. "There's nothing wrong. Only—would you mind very much telling me where you got this five dollar bill?"

The storekeeper took the bill, turned it over, screwed up his features in a grimace evidently meant to intimate deep thought and scratched his head doubtfully.

Billie held her breath and watched him. Everything—simply everything—depended upon this man's memory!

"Well, you know, Miss, it's not so easy to remember who gave you a certain bill when you're busy waiting on customers and making change all day long," he drawled. "Now, there's been quite a lot of customers in here to-day, and how could I know who gave me that particular five dollar bill?"

"Oh, certainly," Billie breathed, "you *must* remember who gave you that bill!"

The dull face of the storekeeper brightened.

"That's right! Come to think of it, I do remember. That cracked peddler, Dan Larkin, give it to me. I recollect because I noticed that big black blot on it at the time."

Billie's heart pounded so loudly she was afraid the storekeeper must hear it. She controlled her excitement sufficiently to ask in a quiet voice:

"Who, if you please, is Dan Larkin?"

"I just told you," said the man peering at her over his spectacles. "Dan Larkin's a queer old chap who keeps a store on wheels. He goes about, stopping at various places and selling things on the way."

"A traveling store," echoed Billie, fighting against disappointment. "Then he isn't here any more?"

"Reckon he is," said the storekeeper carelessly. He had evidently lost interest in the subject. "Dan give me that bill only this morning. He'll probably stick around town all the rest of to-day, anyway."

Billie's hopes soared again.

"I'd consider it a great favor," she said, with her very best smile, "if you could tell me where I am likely to find this—this Dan Larkin."

"He generally parks his van right outside the town limits near the Derry farm. Folks generally know when he's there and go to buy of him."

Billie thanked the storekeeper for this precious information and fairly ran out to the street.

The bent old fellow peered after her and thoughtfully scratched his head.

"Girls are queer creatures," he philosophized. "Now, what in the world does she want to go seeing Dan Larkin for? The way she rushed out into the street, you'd think her life depended on it. It does beat all."

Billie had heard of the Derry farm. It was situated on the outskirts of town. It had long been deserted and the rambling old homestead was said by some to be haunted.

Billie might have walked, but, such was her impatience, she hailed the nearest street car. No time was to be lost! She opened her purse to make sure the five dollar bill with the dark irregular blot across its face was still there.

"The clue!" she murmured, a strange gleam in her eye. "If it only turns out to be the right one!"

Billie left the street car on the edge of town and walked down a country lane. At the end of it was a queer contraption on wheels, a covered motor truck with windows cut in it and a door at the back. This was, undoubtedly, Dan Larkin's traveling store.

Billie hurried forward. Before the rude, ladder-like steps of the "store" she hesitated, but voices from within reassured her.

Dan Larkin was dealing with a customer. He was wrapping up a large parcel when Billie Bradley entered.

The customer lingered, exchanging reminiscences with the grizzled old fellow behind the counter. She went at last, however, and Billie fumbled in her purse for the stained five dollar bill.

She thrust this across the counter toward Dan Larkin.

"Please!" she cried eagerly, "can you tell me where you got that bill?"

CHAPTER XXIII
DAN LARKIN REMEMBERS

DAN LARKIN was a character. He stood behind the little counter of his traveling store, sleeves rolled up to display sinewy forearms, small, good-humored eyes twinkling out from masses of puffy flesh, and a derby hat set rakishly on the back of his grizzled head.

He looked from the bill in Billie's hand to Billie's face and shook his head waggishly.

"You oughtn't to startle an old feller like that," he said. "I ain't sure where I got that bill, young lady—let's see, it's a five dollar one, ain't it? But one thing's certain—I come by it honest!"

"I don't doubt it," replied Billie, smiling engagingly. "Anyone would know you were honest, just to look at you."

"Would they now!" exclaimed the old man delightedly. "That's the best news I've heard in a powerful long time. I *am* honest you know—as the day!"

"I'm sure of it," Billie repeated. "Mr. Larkin," pushing the bill toward him again, "won't you please look at this again closely and tell me if you don't notice anything strange about it?"

"Hm!" said the old man, giving her an extraordinarily shrewd glance from his little, good-humored eyes. "Important, is it?"

"Oh, very, very important!" said Billie.

She waited in an agony of impatience, of mingled hope and fear, while the old man removed one pair of spectacles and replaced them by another. Taking the bill in his hand he peered intently at it.

"A five dollar bill, eh—*with* a blot on it," he ruminated. "Now, what's to be made of that?"

For a long moment he appeared lost in thought, then, with a gesture of regret, pushed the bill across the counter toward Billie.

"Sorry I don't seem to recollect——" Then, as Billie's fingers reached for the bill: "Whoa there! Hold your horses! Sure, I know who give me that five dollars with the spot onto it." The blue eyes twinkled and danced at Billie from between mounds of flesh. "'Twas Mrs. Maria Tatgood. That's who 'twas!"

The interior of that quaint place reeled before Billie. She clung to the counter and heard her voice say faintly, joyfully:

"Has—has Mrs. Maria Tatgood been buying much of you lately?"

"Ho! That's a queer question! But I'll answer it honestly. That's my way. Now you come to speak of it, Mrs. Tatgood has been buying quite a lot of me lately."

"More than she used to?" Billie persisted.

"Quite a good deal more." The small eyes beamed and danced at her. "Yes, I should say she's buying quite a good deal more than usual these days. Which is gratifying to an old chap who has to make his living trundling a store about on wheels. Ain't it, now?"

Billie agreed that it was and, reminded of her own deep obligation to Dan Larkin, she emulated the good example of Mrs. Tatgood and bought several things of him, all of which she could have done very well without.

Scarcely able to believe in her good fortune, Billie returned as quickly as possible to Three Towers Hall. All during the ride in the street car she debated the question as to whether it would be wise to confide her extraordinary news to Laura and Vi.

"Not just yet," was her decision. "Monday and Tuesday are the days of the tennis tournament. I'll wait till after that. Meantime," imitating Mr. Dan Larkin, "I'll keep my eyes open. Oh, won't I just!"

The next day Billie went about radiating so much joyfulness that her chums were curious. Some of them even went so far as to be suspicious.

"Billie Bradley looks like the cat who has just swallowed the canary," said Jessie Brewer. "I wonder," musingly, "if she *could* have had a hand in the disappearance of that Gift Club money!"

"Don't be a goose!" said her companion shortly. "Billie Bradley would never steal anything!"

However, the seed of doubt had been planted, and it grew!

Toward the end of the long pleasant Sunday, Billie's mood of optimism began to wane somewhat. After all, argued the still, small voice of her pessimism, even though she had turned up a red-hot clue, what right had she to believe that she would be able to follow it through to a successful conclusion? It was not a very convincing clue, she told herself, and she was not very experienced in running down clues or trails of any kind.

If only to-morrow were not the beginning of the tennis tournament! If only—if only——

That night Laura and Vi worked over Billie's knee, rubbing, massaging, as earnest in their ministrations as any professional trainer.

"I think it will do now," said Billie, at last. "Thanks so much, girls."

"But how does the knee feel?" Laura insisted.

"All right, most of the time. Then once in a while when I least expect it, it grows a peculiar kink. I can't quite explain it, but suddenly all the strength goes out of it and I feel as though I'd either have to sit down or take a nose dive. Never mind!" smiling at their serious faces, "let's hope it will last through to-morrow. That's all I ask of it!"

"That's all you ask of it, yes," grumbled Vi. "But that's an awful lot to ask of a weak knee, Billie. I'm worried about it. If you'd only kept off of it this past week or two, it might be all right now. As it is—why, don't you know that this tournament is important?"

"Don't I know that this tournament is important! Of course I know! Don't be silly, Vi." Then, seeing that Vi looked a little hurt, she went on: "Oh, I'm sorry, honey. But don't worry. It'll turn out all right."

Next day dawned gloomily, with more than a hint of rain in the sky. However, by ten o'clock the sun had come out to stay, the air was crisp and cool—ideal tennis weather.

Almost the entire student body of Three Towers flocked out upon the grounds. Lessons were suspended for the two days of the tournament. The teachers often came to watch a spirited match. It was not unusual for Miss Walters herself to occupy a camp chair close to the courts during the finals.

Billie crashed through the elimination sets, crushing her opponents without mercy.

"There she goes!" cried Vi, gnawing the ends of her fingers in her excitement. "6—0, 6—2, 6—0. Rose is down, and she waves a wicked racket, too. Oh, boy, there's nobody can stand before Billie to-day!"

"Amanda Peabody is doing just as well. I never saw such pretty work in my life. She seems to be top form."

Vi turned toward the quiet voice and saw Ray Carew standing beside her. She regarded the girl steadily for a long moment.

"Sounds to me as if you were rooting for Amanda, Ray. Are you?"

Rachael had the grace to flush. She avoided Vi's direct glance.

"No," she said, and in a moment walked over to join a friend.

When Vi turned again to watch Billie's smashing service, her clever backhand, her choppy, certain net-work, the enthusiasm she had felt before was definitely overshadowed.

"Billie is just throwing away everything she has gained here by sticking to that wretched Edina Tooker. I can't think what she sees in the girl. I never liked her, anyway—not from the very first!"

When Billie limped from the courts after a day of smashing victories, having reached the finals with a defeat of only one game, her first words were of praise for her adversaries.

"They were all good fighters and game losers," she cried, her eyes shining. "Oh, what a day—what a marvelous day! Where's Laura?"

"Here! I just stopped to lace my shoe."

"You've reached the finals, too, haven't you? Marvelous! We'll double against Amanda and Eliza to-morrow."

"But, Billie, how is your knee?"

"Gracious! I haven't had time to think of it. Now you mention it," with an experimental wriggle of the injured member, "it does hurt a little. Nothing to speak of, though. Oh, what a day!"

Next day, the great day of the finals, dawned bright and clear, though with a hint of rain which no one took note of on the western horizon. By ten o'clock the ring about the courts was packed solid with spectators.

Billie, warming up her service with Laura, vainly searched the ring of faces for Edina Tooker.

"Hiding up in the dormitory, eating her heart out, poor kid," thought Billie, and dubbed her ball into the net.

"Hey, Billie!" Laura shouted. "Stop your daydreaming and send me the ball. I can't pose for the Statue of Liberty all day. My arm waxeth weary."

For revenge Billie patted a ball neatly over her head. Laura swung wildly for it and missed, while a ripple of merriment swept the audience.

"All right for you," called Laura, good-naturedly. "I'll get even with you yet!"

Soon after that the real business of the day commenced.

Billie in the singles, Billie and Laura in the doubles, swiftly eliminated all their adversaries except Amanda Peabody and Eliza Dilks.

Then these two girls went down to a decided but in no sense ignominious defeat before the combined powers of Billie and Laura.

When Billie at last faced Amanda Peabody for the last and deciding match of the tournament, an audible sigh broke from the spectators.

"Now," said Rose Belser, "we are about to see something!"

"It will be a battle of the century," predicted Connie Danvers.

On the courts Billie waved good-naturedly to Amanda.

"Your serve," she called. "Ready?"

CHAPTER XXIV
A SMASHING SET

AMANDA PEABODY had won first serve and her choice of courts. Billie Bradley was handicapped not only by her knee—which was beginning to pain rather severely—but by the fact that the sun was in her eyes.

As Amanda slowly raised her racket for the serve, there was a pleased look on her face. She, too, had noticed Billie's limp and her loss in speed.

"Ready!" she called.

The ball floated over the net lazily. It looked like an easy one, but Billie knew that serve of old. The ball had a tantalizing habit of stopping far short of that part of the court where you expected it.

Billie was ready and returned the ball neatly just over the net. Amanda raced for it, caught it with a clever, backhand stroke, and dropped it over the net. Billie swung at it viciously and sent it sailing over Amanda's head for her first point.

"That was good, wasn't it?" called Billie.

Amanda nodded sullenly.

"Fifteen love!" sang Billie, and set herself for the serve.

From that moment the match settled into one of the grimmest contests ever witnessed on the tennis courts of Three Towers Hall.

Each point was contested fiercely. Amanda and Billie were all over the courts at once; they swung at the ball as though it were a personal enemy; they caressed it deftly into incredible shots that left the spectators mute and tingling with admiration.

"I don't much care who wins," cried Connie Danvers, dancing wildly on the sidelines. "I don't care! I don't care! This is an exhibition worth waiting a hundred years to see. Go it, Billie! Oh boy, what a back hand! Ah—Amanda's got it."

"Forty-thirty," cried Amanda, with a triumphant grin.

The score in games stood five-four in favor of Amanda. Now she needed only one point to win game and set.

It was Amanda's serve. Cunningly, she changed her tactics at this critical moment, hoping to catch Billie off guard. Instead of her usual lazy, tricky serve, she sent a smashing ball over the net, carrying it far into the back court.

Billie raced for it, forgetting her injured knee, caught the ball by little less than a miracle of skill, returned it, just missing the top of the net.

Amanda slipped it over neatly and Billie had to run for it again.

On the sidelines Vi wailed:

"She'll never last it, Laura! Her poor knee! How does she do it?"

"But she does it!" shrieked Laura, her eyes on fire. "Vi, look at that return! She's got Amanda on the run now! Go it, Billie—go it!"

Billie, knowing that she must save her knee, played close to the net. Never so cool as in an emergency, she juggled the ball, sent Amanda dashing all over the courts like a puppet at the end of a string.

It was such a masterly display as the girls had seldom seen. They were on their feet, shouting, groaning, stamping with their feet.

Billie, cool, steady, saw her opportunity. Amanda, red and perspiring, danced around in the back court, expecting a smashing return.

Billie ran backward, caught the ball neatly on the tip of her racket, landed it teasingly, gently, just inside the net.

Amanda made a gallant dash for it, swung for it, and swooped up a handful of sod on her racket.

"Forty-all," said Billie and added generously: "Well tried, Amanda."

That was practically the end of the match, so far as Amanda was concerned. At best, a temperamental, erratic player, she was hopeless when mastered by fury. Now she forgot all the skill and artistry of her game, sent smashing shots to Billie that the latter returned with ease.

Billie won that game, making it five-all, and took the next two on points.

Amanda flung down her racket and followed it from the courts without pausing to shake hands with her successful rival.

Those from the sidelines thronged about Billie, showering her with compliments, dwelling on those few moments at the net when she had showed her complete mastery of the game.

"I never saw such marvelous form!"

"But, Billie, what makes you limp so?"

"Billie may limp, but her game doesn't!"

The praise was sweet to Billie. She drank it in eagerly, knowing that, for that moment at least, all grudges were forgotten and she was once more first in the hearts of her fellow students.

Espying Edina Tooker on the fringe of the crowd, Billie broke away from the adulation of her schoolmates and went straight to the girl. That glimpse of Edina had served to remind Billie that she was at last free to resume her investigations in the girl's behalf, to continue the attempt to fasten the guilt for the theft of the Gift Club fund upon the real thief and so absolve Edina.

From the courts, her friends watched Billie greet the ostracized girl and a queer silence settled over them. They were remembering their grievance against Billie Bradley. It was as though a damp cloud settled on their spirits, obliterating their enthusiasm.

"I must say," sniffed someone in the group, "I think Billie might be less open in her friendship with that horrid girl. I can't think how she can still cling to her!"

Edina met Billie with outstretched hands.

"You were wonderful!" she cried. "I had to come out. I knew I oughtn't to, but I had to see you beat Amanda Peabody. If I could play tennis like that!"

"Maybe you will some day," replied Billie.

Edina caught her up quickly.

"Some day! I'm not going to be here that long, Billie. I've got to get away from here—and get away quick."

"That's what I want to talk to you about. Come away with me, Edina. I have something to tell you that I think will interest you greatly."

"May we come, too?" The voice was Laura Jordon's who, with Vi, had come up so quietly they had not been observed.

"Of course!" cried Billie eagerly. "I wasn't sure you'd care to hear what I have to say. But I think you will like it—*when* you hear it. Come along!"

The four girls walked for some distance into the woods along the lakeshore. Then, making sure they were not observed, Billie recounted for the benefit of her interested audience the story of her adventurous day in town and the identification of the smudged five dollar bill by Dan Larkin.

"You see," she explained, "that five dollar bill with the ink blot on it was part of my contribution to the Gift Club fund. I remember noticing it at the time and thinking that it was a pity to have to give in such a soiled-looking bill. When I recognized it that day in town I decided to trace it back in the hope of finding a clue to the person who stole the rest of the Gift Club money."

"Did you?" breathed Vi.

"Did I? Listen! I found that an old peddler by the name of Dan Larkin had given the bill to my storekeeper and when I followed up that lead, who do you suppose I found had given the bill to Dan Larkin? A Mrs. Tatgood!"

"Tatgood!" repeated Laura. "Why, that's the name of one of the dormitory maids, isn't it?"

"Maria Tatgood has charge of Edina's dormitory," Billie pointed out. "The Mrs. Tatgood mentioned by Dan Larkin must be some relative, her mother perhaps."

"But, Billie, if you think this Mrs. Tatgood is the thief, shouldn't we notify the police?"

"I thought of that the first thing," Billie confessed. "But, after all, we have only suspicions to go on so far. What the police want is proof."

"Then why not get busy and produce the proof?" cried Laura.

"Exactly! We may have to call in the boys to help. In fact, I think it would be a good idea to ask their help. We may need it."

Vi, who had been eying Billie thoughtfully, blurted out:

"You have some definite plan in mind, Billie. I can tell by the look of you. Come clean now. What is it?"

"Well, I'll tell you."

Whereupon Billie outlined her plan. It was that she and Laura and Vi, Edina too, if she liked, would enter into a plot to search Maria Tatgood's room.

"Vi and I will look through the maid's things—she is almost certain to have some of the money hidden about the house—while you and Edina, Laura, keep watch to see that we are not interrupted."

"Now is a good time," Vi suggested. "Nearly everybody is still on the courts discussing the tournament. Whatever we do will be likely to pass unnoticed."

"All right. Come ahead!" replied Billie.

The four girls returned to the Hall, entered cautiously by the rear way, and went directly to the servants' quarters, where they found Maria Tatgood's room without difficulty.

Billie tried the door and found it unlocked. Feeling like the most desperate of conspirators, she opened the door and slipped inside, motioning to Vi to follow her.

"We'll have to be quick," she whispered. "Maria may come back at any time."

The room contained a bed, a dresser, a washstand, two chairs and a trunk.

"You take the dresser," Billie directed. "I'll attend to the trunk."

The trunk was opened, but on lifting the lid, Billie found it almost empty. A brief search served to assure her that nothing was there.

Vi had a little luck with the dresser. She unearthed fifteen dollars in bills, but at sight of them Billie shook her head in disappointment.

"No good, if we don't find more than that," she said.

At the moment there came a soft, insistent scratching at the door, the agreed-upon signal that trouble was brewing.

Billie slammed down the trunk lid. Vi shoved things into the dresser drawer. Outside the room they found Laura and Edina in an agony of impatience.

"Some one is coming! Hurry!"

They whisked about a turn in the corridor just in time to avoid the person whose room they had ransacked. Careful to keep themselves hidden, they watched Maria Tatgood go into her room and shut the door.

When Billie's companions would have slipped away, anxious to get back to the dormitory, she detained them.

"Let's watch for awhile," she proposed. "We may see something of interest. You never can tell."

Billie afterwards said that her suggestion was prompted by a "hunch." Be that as it may, the fact remains that Maria Tatgood emerged from her room almost immediately, wearing hat and coat as though ready for an outing. She turned down the corridor toward the servants' entrance to the Hall.

"Come along!" said Billie impulsively. "Let's follow her!"

CHAPTER XXV
CAUGHT—CONCLUSION

BILLIE BRADLEY and her three companions were without wraps, though they were too excited to think of that. Also, they had had no time to inform the boys at Boxton Military Academy as to their purpose and enlist their help. They were too excited to think of that, either.

They followed Maria Tatgood, always at a discreet distance, through the school gates and along the dusty road.

"Where do you suppose she's going?" Laura whispered.

"Home!" said Billie "I've a notion we are going to make a real discovery this time!"

Maria Tatgood lived in an old house, set well back from the road and surrounded by tall trees. There had been no attempt to cut the grass that grew in reedy abundance to the very steps of the porch. The house itself was in a state of considerable disrepair. A little carpentry work and a coat or two of paint would have made it a much more habitable place.

All these things impressed themselves more or less vividly on the minds of the girls as they watched Maria Tatgood ascend the worn steps of the porch and disappear into the house.

The day had turned dismal and chill. The sun had disappeared under the clouds that by this time had risen from a streak low on the western horizon and covered the zenith. A light, misty rain was falling. There among the trees it was gloomy and dark.

Evidently, the occupants of the house were also in semi-darkness, for, as the girls watched, they saw a light flash up in a room at the rear. From this same room presently came the sound of angry voices.

Billie tugged Vi's sleeve.

"Come along! Tell Laura and Edina. The folks inside have forgotten to pull the shade down at that window. Thanks to them, we can both see and hear."

Silently, keeping to the shelter of the trees, the girls crept toward that lighted window. The angry voices were becoming intelligible. The girls could hear phrases, scraps of sentences.

"You've spent it! You had no business——"

"I had no business, didn't I? I like that! Ain't I your mother?"

Billie put finger to lips in a gesture of caution and crept closer to the window. Laura pinched Vi's arm. Edina's face looked very white in the dusk.

"Just the same," came the younger voice sullenly, "you ain't keepin' to your end of the bargain. We was to split, wasn't we?"

"Split, is it?" The voice of the older woman rose waspishly. "I should have the big half, anyways. Ain't I your mother?"

"It was me took all the risks. It was that way in the old days, too, wasn't it? It was me opened the pocketbooks of the rich women in the stores while you took the money I got out of 'em! Well, it ain't goin' to be so no more. We split, or I quit!"

A sullen silence fell upon the room and its occupants. Outside the girls held their breath to listen. After a moment the more youthful voice continued:

"How much you got left of the money?"

"Two hundred dollars. That's all exceptin' a few cents in silver—a half a dollar, maybe."

"You've already spent sixty dollars? Well, if that ain't a rum go!"

Suddenly Edina clutched Billie's arm.

"Quick! Hide!" she cried. "Somebody's comin'!"

The watchers had barely time to gain the shelter of the trees when a thick-set figure loomed up through the gloom. A man brushed past them, a man with hunched shoulders and a week's growth of stubble on his face.

This person stumped around to the rear of the house, a door opened and closed, and soon the two voices within the room were joined by a third.

"Hello, you cats at it ag'in, scratchin' and clawin'? Where's my dinner? That's what I'd like to know. When are you goin' to git me some grub?"

Billie turned to her companions. They could see her eyes shining in the dull light.

"We've heard enough!" she whispered. "Let's be getting back."

They fairly ran down the road to Three Towers Hall. They were scarcely aware that they were cold and dishevelled and pretty well soaked by the misty drizzle. In their minds two facts loomed paramount. They had positively identified Maria Tatgood as the thief, and two hundred dollars of the Gift Club fund still remained in the custody of the unsavory Tatgood family. If they hurried, they still might save that two hundred dollars.

Up the steps of the school they rushed and into the hall, to be met by a group of horrified girls.

"Where have you been?"

"To the wars, if looks count for anything!"

"You big sillies! You are soaked through!"

Connie Danvers pushed through the crowd and plucked Billie anxiously by the sleeve.

"Listen! Eliza Dilks saw you girls leave by the front gate a little while ago. She reported to Amanda. Of course Amanda promptly reported to Miss Walters. She's up there in Miss Walters' office now. I'm afraid you are in for it, Billie!"

"Where are you going?" she added, as Billie broke from her and made for the stairs.

From the first step Billie looked down upon the group of curious, upturned faces.

"I am going to see Miss Walters on an important mission," she said, with a challenging laugh. "You may come, too, if you like!"

Many of the girls availed themselves of this permission and trooped after her. There was a mysterious air about Billie Bradley and her companions that roused their curiosity and warned them to expect developments of an extraordinary character.

The group was joined on the way by new recruits, so by the time Billie and her friends reached the door of Miss Walters' office about half the student body was trailing at her heels.

"You all wait here," said Billie to her escort. "I'll leave the door open just a crack so that you can hear what happens."

Billie tapped on the door of the office. After a brief pause, Miss Walters' pleasant voice called, "Come in!"

As Billie pushed open the door she gestured to Vi and Laura and Edina to follow her.

"I can see Amanda in there," she whispered. "I don't intend to take my medicine alone!"

Miss Walters looked up as the girls entered. The troubled frown on her face deepened.

"Amanda has just been telling me about you," she said, tapping her desk with a pencil. "Did you four students leave these grounds without permission?"

"Yes, Miss Walters," said Billie meekly, and added unnecessarily: "We have just got back."

"So it seems!" Miss Walters' frown deepened. She continued the ra-ta-ta-tat with the pencil on the edge of her desk. Amanda's triumphant smirk grew until it seemed to spread over all of her face.

"You have some explanation?" said Miss Walters, at last.

This was the opportunity for which Billie had waited. Making sure that the door of the office was open so that the girls outside could hear everything she said, she addressed the white-haired, gracious head of Three Towers Hall.

"Miss Walters, I have an explanation. When you hear it I think you will forgive us for leaving the grounds without asking permission."

Miss Walters inclined her head, half-smiling at Billie's earnestness.

"Let me hear the explanation," she said.

Billie drew a long breath and plunged into her story. She began with the founding of the Gift Club and Edina's elevation to the post of treasurer. She went on through the strange disappearance of the Gift Club fund, dwelling upon Edina Tooker's distress upon finding herself suspected of the theft.

When she came to the account of her day in town, including the identification of the blotted five dollar bill, Miss Walters' interest visibly increased. There was an audible sigh from the girls grouped close about the office door. Amanda's triumphant grin grew slightly less triumphant.

"So you see, the evidence all pointed to the dormitory maid, Maria Tatgood," Billie pleaded.

Miss Walters nodded.

"Yes," she said, "I see. Please go on."

"Well, when we saw Maria leave the Hall to-night we felt that there, perhaps, was the chance to establish real evidence—police evidence—against her. We should have asked your permission, Miss Walters, to leave the school grounds, but we really hadn't time."

Billie was still pleading her case. Miss Walters nodded as though she understood—as, indeed, she did.

"Go on!"

As Billie proceeded she was vividly aware of the keen interest that greeted her account of the happenings leading up to the positive identification of Maria Tatgood as the thief.

At the startling revelation Amanda's jaw dropped open. Billie, happening to glance at her, choked back a laugh, which brought on such a dire attack of coughing and strangling that Miss Walters inquired with a smile on her own lips whether she would not feel better for a glass of water.

"No, th-thanks," stuttered Billie. "I—I'm all right now."

"About this Maria Tatgood," said Miss Walters, her face suddenly stern. "If your story is to be trusted—and I have never yet found occasion to question any statement of yours—then this Maria Tatgood and her infamous family must be brought to the attention of the police, and at once. I will attend to it."

Miss Walters was silent for a moment, tracing thoughtful figures on a scrap of paper. When she looked up the troubled frown had completely vanished from her face.

"You left the school grounds without permission, which is against the rules and so merits rebuke."

"Yes, Miss Walters," murmured Billie, her eyes demurely lowered.

"However," continued the principal in her pleasant, flowing voice, "your conduct was prompted by such exemplary motives that I am tempted to waive punishment for this time. In fact," Miss Walters flung out her hand toward Billie in a gracious, impulsive gesture, "I must congratulate you, my dear girl, on the persistent loyalty and friendliness you have shown toward Edina Tooker, this sorely misunderstood girl. You are a friend such as I would choose for myself."

This praise flooded Billie with an emotion that robbed her of words. She could only look her love and gratitude.

Miss Walters said softly:

"Edina! Edina Tooker, come here, my dear."

Edina approached uncertainly and stood before the gracious, white-haired lady who held her own fate and the fate of all the students of Three Towers Hall in the hollow of her hand.

Miss Walters searched among the papers on her desk and drew forth a letter.

"This communication came to me to-day, Edina. It is from your father and it contains news that I am sure you will be glad to hear."

Edina looked big and awkward and pitiful as she stood there, nervously twisting her fingers together.

"Your father has struck oil again on his property—a genuine gusher this time. I imagine you will be very, very rich, Edina."

Miss Walters smiled, as though at some secret thought of her own. Reaching into the letter she drew forth a long yellow slip.

"Your father asked me to give you this check—to help him celebrate, he said."

Edina took the slip of paper without pausing to read the illiterate scrawl across its face. Her eyes were on Miss Walters' face.

"You been so awful good to me," she muttered.

"You are worth being good to, Edina," said Miss Walters, smiling. "Billie and I have always believed that—haven't we, Billie?"

Miss Walters held out a hand and Edina slipped her clumsy red one into it. At the touch, all the iron in Edina's nature suddenly melted before a turbulent flood of emotion.

She flung herself to her knees beside Miss Walters, and buried her face in her lap, harsh sobs tore at her aching throat.

Miss Walters stroked the dark hair and glanced with gentle meaning at the other girls.

"You may go now," she said. "I'll send Edina down to you. She will feel better presently."

As the girls passed from the office to be met by a group of deeply moved and silenced students in the outer hall, Amanda Peabody was heard to mutter vindictively:

"Billie Bradley has all the pull in this place! She can get away with anything!"

It was the night of the big dance at Boxton Military Academy. Billie was there and Laura and Vi and, yes—oh, of course—Edina Tooker.

Billie was a dream—Teddy told her so—in a rose-colored chiffon evening dress. Scarcely less lovely were Laura in a dainty lavender chiffon dress and Vi in a clinging crêpe that brought out her pretty figure to perfection.

Edina in her gold-colored taffeta with gold slippers on her feet, her hair a shining, blue-black cap for her shapely head, was quite the rage with the young cadets at Boxton. She could not dance very well, but she was learning. In truth, there appeared to be no dearth of dancing instructors, prominent among these being the good-looking Paul Martinson.

Billie and her chums discussed these—and other things—during a temporary lull in the festivities. Teddy and Chet and Ferd Stowing had gone to fetch ice-cream and some of those "ducky little almond-flavored cakes."

"Well," said Laura as she patted a soft bow of her chiffon frock into place, "I can only remark what I believe a gentleman called Shakespeare has already remarked before me, 'All's well that ends well!'"

"Which sentiment we echo heartily," agreed Billie. "I crave your indulgence for a moment while I sum up our reasons for gratitude. First of all, Maria Tatgood and her mother are safe in jail where they will steal no more Gift Club funds. The two hundred dollars has been recovered——"

"It was generous of Edina to make up the missing sixty dollars from the check her father sent her," interpolated Vi.

"Well, Edina has plenty of money now, you know. She'll never miss that sixty dollars. Paw Tooker will probably be a millionaire before his new gusher stops gushing, and what's Paw's seems to belong equally to his beloved Edina. But to continue with the list of our blessings. With the two hundred and sixty dollars, we have been able to buy Miss Geraldine Gay a most gorgeous wedding present——"

"She was delighted with it, wasn't she?"

"Why wouldn't she be? There is no finer grandfather's clock around here."

"When is she to be married?"

"Not before the Thanksgiving holidays. The new teacher comes then."

"That's not so far away. We're not too awfully forehanded with our gift."

"To continue with the list of our blessings," reiterated Billie dreamily: "Our friend and fellow student, Violet Farrington, has recovered from her backslidings in math to the extent of working off an onerous condition——"

"And it *is* a blessing, believe me!" said Vi fervently. "With that condition off my shoulders, I feel as though I could begin to look about and enjoy myself."

"Here come the boys with our ice-cream."

"I hope they have brought dozens of cakes!"

"Before they get here," said Laura hurriedly, "there is just one little point I'd like cleared up."

"Any little thing we can do," murmured Billie.

"It's about that five dollar gold piece that Edina spent in the shoe shop to buy a pair of shoes. If that was Nellie Bane's five dollar gold piece——"

"It wasn't. It was Edina's. She had kept it as a lucky piece but, being short of funds, was forced to use it to buy shoes. Any more questions?"

"How about Nellie's gold piece, then?"

"It was part of the sixty dollars spent by Maria Tatgood's mother; she admitted as much when pressed. Now, no more questions, please. Let joy be unconfined!"

"It is a lovely party, isn't it?" breathed Vi.

With her eyes on Edina Tooker's happy face, Billie Bradley answered:

"Yes, it is. The very nicest, ever!"

THE END

Milton Keynes UK
Ingram Content Group UK Ltd.
UKHW040900050124
435493UK00006B/965